PENGUI
THE TUNN

Rasipuram Krishnaswamy Laxman was born and educated in Mysore. Soon after he graduated from the University of Mysore, he started drawing cartoons for the *Free Press Journal,* a newspaper in Bombay. Six months later he joined the *Times of India,* a newspaper he has been with, as staff cartoonist, for over fifty years. He has written and published numerous short stories, essays and travel articles. Some of these were published in a book, *Idle Hours*. He has also written two novels, *The Hotel Riviera* and *The Messenger,* both published by Penguin Books. Penguin has also published several collections of Laxman's cartoons in the series *The Best of Laxman* and *Laugh with Laxman.* In June 1998, the *Times of India* published a collection entitled *50 Years of Independence Through the Eyes of R.K. Laxman.*

R.K. Laxman was awarded the prestigious Padma Bhushan by the Government of India. The University of Marathwada conferred an honorary Doctor of Literature degree on him. He has won many awards for his cartoons, including Asia's top journalism award, the Ramon Magsaysay Award, in 1984.

The Tunnel of Time

An Autobiography

R. K. Laxman

PENGUIN BOOKS

PENGUIN BOOKS
Published by the Penguin Group
Penguin Books India Pvt Ltd, 11 Community Centre, Panchsheel Park, New Delhi 110 017, India
Penguin Group (USA) Inc., 375 Hudson Street, New York, New York 10014, USA
Penguin Group (Canada), 90 Eglinton Avenue East, Suite 700, Toronto, Ontario, M4P 2Y3, Canada (a division of Pearson Penguin Canada Inc.)
Penguin Books Ltd, 80 Strand, London WC2R 0RL, England
Penguin, Ireland, 25 St Stephen's Green, Dublin 2, Ireland (a division of Penguin Books Ltd)
Penguin Group (Australia), 250 Camberwell Road, Camberwell, Victoria 3124, Australia (a division of Pearson Australia Group Pty Ltd)
Penguin Group (NZ), cnr Airborne and Rosedale Roads, Albany, Auckland 1310, New Zealand (a division of Pearson New Zealand Ltd)
Penguin Group (South Africa) (Pty) Ltd, 24 Sturdee Avenue, Rosebank, Johannesburg 2196, South Africa

Penguin Books Ltd, Registered Offices: 80 Strand, London WC2R 0RL, England

First published in Viking by Penguin Books India 1998
Published in Penguin Books 1999

10 9 8 7 6 5

Typeset in Times Roman by Digital Technologies and Printing Solutions, New Delhi
Printed at DeUnique Printers, New Delhi

Dedicated to the
memory of my parents

This is not an autobiography in the usual sense. If I think I am writing one I become too self-conscious, and my style of narration gets stifled. Besides, I keep neither diary nor calendar and I have never worn a watch! So, without fumbling for dates and times, I plan to ramble on, taking help from my memory for what it is worth, recounting my experiences, reactions and anecdotes, and describing people I have met and places I have visited. All these are the normal contents of anyone's life and in my case they moulded me into a satirical cartoonist.

I do not remember wanting to do anything else except draw. Draw pictures as a child, as a boy, as a youth in college and later in life, as a professional illustrator, draw politicians, distort their faces and ridicule their comments graphically for a living. Of course, I had kicked a football on the field and hit a ball with a bat creditably on the cricket pitch in my school and college days, but never had I put my heart into these activities. My passion was sketching: street scenes, people and landscapes. I do not remember a day when I have not sketched, whether it was the time to prepare for examinations or lying in bed recovering from a bout of fever. I had no aspiration to be an engine driver, a doctor, a lawyer or a management consultant as a child.

An artist, that was what I wanted to be. I found learning arithmetic, geometry, geography, languages somewhat an intrusion into my natural pursuit of sitting on a bench in the market square with my sketch book, observing people and recording my impressions. I decided that I would pass my examinations but I never attempted to get high marks. Thus

I divided my time evenly between the compulsory demands of the classroom and my inner urge to improve my talent. My parents and elders were a great help, for they never took it seriously when one of their sons got pitiably low marks or even failed!

I was the youngest of six sons. One or the other was always failing exams; we stumbled along without any fear that Father would fume and fret and erupt like a volcano. He was that sort of a person. All over Mysore he had the reputation of being the strictest headmaster, who laid down an exacting code of conduct for his students. It was said that all those who later succeeded in life had passed through the ordeal of the cane at my father's hands!

I was very young when he passed away. He had the bearing and appearance of a Roman senator—grim, with a permanent expression of disapproval.

His pastime was reading and our house was full of books he used to get from England. He also used to play a bit of tennis at the Cosmopolitan Club in the evenings. He had a profound knowledge of Carnatic music and often quietly played the veena, strictly for his inner joy.

But these details of his personal life were little known to his colleagues and the clerical staff at the high school. They dreaded his temper and discreetly vanished round corners or behind pillars at his approach. He was nicknamed 'The Tiger'.

It was said that one of the clerks in his office fainted when my father looked straight into his eyes questioningly when he discovered a broken official seal on an envelope containing some confidential papers. Then it seems they had to hold the poor fellow's head and douche cold water on his face to revive him!

Yet it was amazing that such a man was so tolerant when one or the other of his sons failed in an examination.

I think it was my mother who had the taming influence at home. She was quite the opposite of my father in nature: fond of company and of cheerful disposition. Besides being a good tennis player, she was very proficient in bridge and almost a champion in chess! Once or twice a week she attended the Maharani Ladies Club.

Her absence didn't bother me. I used to play quietly with the brothers close to me in age. But as darkness fell I would ask for her and start missing her each passing minute. Then, slowly I would become the centre of concern for the servant, the cook and the other elders of the household and attempts would be made variously to keep me engaged and stop me from crying. Then there would be the sound of a car stopping at the gate, announcing the arrival of Mother. I would rush to the veranda and jump with joy as if I had not seen her for ages. But not all days ended happily thus.

Her Highness the Maharani of Mysore was a regular visitor to the club. Some days she would corner my mother to play a game of chess. She was a poor player, pondering over each move with a lot of delay, doubt and deliberation. In deference to the royal opponent my mother feigned appropriate caution and concentration while she made her moves. All this used to take the game well past the club's closing hours, which of course did not apply to the Maharani whom my mother would allow finally to triumph. Then Mother would be invited to dinner at the palace. By this time I would have become uncontrollable at home, screaming for my mother. The rest of the household too would catch the mood and hang about the windows anxiously looking for the arrival of the palace car. Father would be rumbling like a volcano with supressed rage, steadily watching the darkness outside through the window, arms akimbo, legs apart.

On such days my brother Seenu took charge of me, and whistled soft tunes, drawing profiles of men and women at the same time, brilliant sketches on sheets of paper, figures of people running, walking, bending, carrying loads on their heads, and so on. I used to sit hypnotized beside him in the chair, eyes transfixed on the magic of creation. The whole house would heave a sigh of relief when the car arrived and Mother came up the steps, followed by palace guards in uniform bearing trays full of sweets, dry nuts and fresh fruit. At the sight of these delicacies Father's wrath would melt away yielding to a faint smile. He would then pick up a sweet, pop it into his mouth and retire to his room, munching.

My parents somehow did not realize that it was time I should be sent to school! Left to myself all day, I played around the house merrily. My brothers having gone to college or school, Father taking a walk or visiting bookshops, and Mother busy in the kitchen or in the pooja room, I enjoyed roaming in the large empty hall and rooms all by myself without elders' interference. Anything that caught my fancy I used to draw on the floor with a piece of chalk. Sometimes I tried the effect of a pencil stub on the whitewashed walls.

This paradise came to an abrupt stop one day when one of my uncles visiting us from Madras found me playing at the odd hour of nine in the morning, when all the other children of my age had already been in their classes for over an hour.

When he learnt that I had no clue to school or studies he picked me up unceremoniously and carried me to a nearby primary municipal school. I kicked and cried my heart out all the way but to no avail. He met the headmaster and told him whose spoilt son I was. I was admitted to the 'A' class immediately. My uncle, having done the job, thanked the headmaster and walked away. I was still crying unashamedly before all the children when I saw my uncle hurrying away. Unrestrained by anyone, I ran after him. He stopped and ordered me back to the class. Then he began to walk away. I followed him at a distance. Again he stopped. I too stopped. He moved. I moved. In this manner we both reached home, where the protective presence of my mother saved me from the uncle and education. After this traumatic experience I resumed my usual freedom at home as before for several months.

A huge case of deal wood in a corner of one of the rooms used to be my personal box. I dumped all my possessions in it—a bicycle chain, a hubcap from a car, a deflated football, a home-made cricket bat, several toy cars with broken mainsprings, any number of tennis balls, empty chocolate boxes and so on. When I was not drawing on the floor I sat right on top of all these odds and ends, burrowed deep into the contents and foraged through my collections, examining each item and playing with it for hours on end.

One day I discovered three broken glass panes. I had picked them up somewhere and hidden them from the elders, for they would never have let me handle objects with such razor-sharp jagged edges. Having secreted them away carefully in the subterranean depths of the box, I had forgotten about them. I treasured them for their scintillating colours—red, blue and green. They offered me a whole world of magic turning the landscape into the colour I fancied when I peeped through them. I was thrilled to see the entire garden—trees, flowers, the gardener, his turban, shirt, bucket—drenched in green. Then I turned the entire vista into grim red and set it aglow like an oven.

After that I quickly turned my surroundings into a moonlit world, ghostly, cold and mysterious, as I peered through the dark blue broken glass. I had discovered an entire universe of romance. I used to transform the landscape from one colour to another, sitting on our garden wall. I remember an old man passing by on the road saw and realized the thrill I was having and said, 'To be young is very heaven, my boy, very heaven . . .' in Kannada. Later in life I discovered it was a quotation from an English poet.

After all these absorbing activities I still found time to look for further diversions. I used to venture into my father's room to examine things there. Several pairs of spectacles—tinted, plain, roundish, oval. There were at least a dozen walking sticks in a corner—malacca canes, ebony sticks with ivory handles, some with the face of a hound, or a silver knob. What really attracted me was the bedside table piled with foreign magazines. I used to gather these, spread them on the floor and go through them one by one. I used to be lost looking at the large black and white illustrations for the stories. My favourite was the *Strand Magazine*. It carried short stories by eminent writers such as P.G. Wodehouse, Arthur Conan Doyle, W.W. Jacob and many others. All of the stories were generously illustrated in minute detail. The other magazines I browsed through were *Bystander*, *Wide World*, *Tit Bits* and of course, *Punch*.

I could not read the jokes under the cartoons, which were in pen and ink by different artists with different styles. But I used to spend hours studying each and would critically judge their quality. This exercise helped me to develop a visual sense of humour and also the rudiments of perspective, drapery and human anatomy, without being conscious of these. One day I was so impressed with one of the cartoons in *Punch* that I sat down with a paper and pencil to copy it. I had hardly started when one of my brothers passing by saw me, stopped in his tracks and said, 'Copying? Never. Look around, observe and sketch! You will never be an artist if you copy. It is like eating leftover food from someone else's plate.' At that time I didn't fully understand the comparison, but the admonition so severely delivered struck home, and scared me out of ever attempting to copy again!

On the whole my days were heavenly indeed, as remarked by the old man who had passed by and seen me playing with my pieces of coloured glass on the garden wall.

At about this time one Chikkannayappa began to visit my brother Narayan regularly each morning. Usually Narayan used to be away attending college, or out for a walk if it happened to be a holiday. But now I found him in the company of this daily visitor, engaged in some discussion.

Through snatches of conversation among the elders I gathered that Chikkannayappa, having failed repeatedly in English in his B.A. exam year after year, came for tuition in English from my brother.

He became a familiar figure, appearing at the gate at the appointed time. He even played with me in the garden, tossing a ball or helping me to fly a kite if Narayan happened to be taking his bath or was busy somewhere inside the house.

On one such day he suddenly stopped playing and asked, looking at his watch, if I did not have a school to go to. When I told him I did not, the same scene that had occured a few months ago repeated itself. Only this time it was Chikkannayappa and not my uncle from Madras who carried me on his shoulders to the municipal primary school. I repeated my performance of crying and kicking but the headmaster, recognizing me, re-admitted me and took a hand this time in preventing me from running after Chikkannayappa when he walked away.

Strangely enough from that day on, I began to attend classes regularly. I even insisted on going to school on Sundays, and returned from the deserted building disappointed. I began to wear a mandatory flat black cap and coat and possessed a slate and piece of chalk to practice the Kannada alphabet. All of us, about twenty boys, sat side by side on rows of long benches. The teacher kept on his table a few pieces of chalk, an attendance register and, most important of all, a cane. Besides the alphabet, we were taught to read and count numbers. We had just one textbook which contained simple sentences such as: 'Rama, stand up. Stand erect. See that garden of banana trees . . .' Each one of us was made to read these lines without stumbling or making mistakes. We also had a section in the same textbook devoted to poems. The one I remember was about a tale of an unfortunate parrot. It went somewhat like this: 'The parrot is not in its cage! Sister, on your advice I raised this little parrot. It played on my palm. It grew wings and learnt to say "Rama, Rama!" Alas! a cat took it away!' I don't know which educationist thought this an edifying lesson for youngsters.

My eyes smarted and became misty whenever I had to recite this sad poem.

Our teacher's appearance conformed to the classic stereotype. He was lean and dark, with untrimmed mossy clumps of hair cascading from his upper lip. One could never see his mouth fully, only his front two teeth which jutted out like a rabbit's when he smiled or grimaced. He wore a turban, a tight coat and what was called a cycle-dhoti—it was wound round in a manner that made the legs resemble narrow drainpipes. A stale smell of beedi hung about him permanently.

When the urge to have a smoke came over him he left the class in charge of his appointee who told us stories to keep us engaged, while the monitor maintained order. The boy narrated the same story, always about the crow and the princes or the crocodile and the monkey or the donkey and the court jester. We did not pay attention as we already knew the stories; we carried on our private gossip in whispers. When the monitor saw a paper dart suddenly hurtle towards him from nowhere, or a piece of chalk fly past like a bullet, he took down the names of the suspects. Later he submitted the list to the teacher, who meanwhile relaxed quietly and satisfied his need behind the toilet block, out of sight of the headmaster, peons and boys. He returned to class trailing the pungent odour of beedi.

One day, instead of leaving the class in charge of the monitor before stepping out to have a couple of puffs, he set us a task: we were ordered to draw a leaf, any leaf.

This was something new and exciting and all the boys at once set about it enthusiastically. We were soon absorbed in the creative task. Some boys sat wondering trying to imagine a leaf. One fellow drew a banana leaf that was so big it went out of the wooden frame of the slate. Another boy, after pondering for a while and failing to visualize a leaf, announced loudly, 'I am going to draw an elephant instead!' Thus we were so busily engaged that we had not even noticed the teacher either leaving or returning. A couple of loud thumps on the table with the cane brought us back to reality.

He asked us to queue up and began to critically examine our efforts one by one, murmuring comments and giving marks. Sometimes he twisted a boy's ear or brought the cane down on the leg of another. When it was my turn, he stared at the drawing for an alarmingly long time and asked me, 'Did you draw it yourself, Laxman?' I was frightened and stepped back, expecting a shower of blows. I replied, 'You asked us to draw, sir . . . I sat there and drew . . .' fumbling for a safe excuse. But to my great surprise and joy he held my slate up before the class and announced, 'Attention! Look how nicely Laxman has drawn the leaf!' He turned to me and said, 'You will be an artist one day. Keep it up.' He gave me ten marks out of ten. He was very impressed by the perfect shape of my peepal leaf and the details of the veins branching out along the midrib. I had seen these leaves countless times strewn on the road under the peepal tree, and I could draw them effortlessly. I was inspired by this unexpected encouragement. I began to think of myself as an artist in the making, never doubting that this was my destiny.

My drawings on the floors, walls and doors of my house began to proliferate. Once I saw Father sitting in a chair and reading a newspaper. His profile, like that of a Roman senator, stood out clearly and the fringe of gray hair circling his bald head like a wreath added to his imposing appearance.

I sketched him on the floor with chalk. My mother who was passing by recognized the caricature. She began to laugh and invited my father to have a look at it! He furiously ordered me to wipe it off at once. Mother insisted it should remain till others came home and saw it too. Finally she prevailed, and the caricature remained on the floor for a long time till it faded and disappeared in the course of time.

School began to be less and less a place for fun, gossip and playing games as I moved year after year from class to class. The lessons became tough and complicated and the teachers were increasingly demanding. I was especially weak in arithmetic. It was a nightmare to have to distribute fifteen mangoes equally among three people. But I was good in history and could name villains and heroes and warriors and identify civilizations and centuries. Similarly I could remember the names of mountains and oceans and rivers in geography.

We read prose which taught us moral values such as truthfulness, honesty, showing respect to elders and so on, expressed through characters in folklore and mythology. The themes of the poems we were taught also urged us to internalize the principles of noble conduct. One of the most powerful poems was about a cow called Punyakoti, grazing along with others of its herd. But Punyakoti somehow strayed on the way back home in the evening. A huge hungry tiger accosted the cow and demanded that she become his meal. Not losing her calm, Punyakoti promised to come back and offer herself as his dinner after suckling her hungry calf. The tiger let her go, but to his utter surprise she was true to her promise and returned after some time. The tiger was so moved by Punyakoti's honesty that he cried bitterly and threw himself from the edge of the cliff.

The other equally unforgettable poem known to all educated Kannadigas of that era was about a woodcutter. One day he accidentally dropped his iron axe into a pond. God wanted to test his honesty. Disguised as a fisherman, God retrieved the axe from the bottom of the pool and gave it back to the woodcutter. But upon finding that the axe was made of gold, the man returned it, saying it was not his. God again plunged into the pool and came up with another axe, this time made of silver, which also was refused by the woodcutter. Finally, when the old iron axe was retrieved and offered, he accepted it with delight. God was pleased with his honesty. Revealing his divine identity, he blessed the woodcutter and rewarded him suitably.

I listened to the teacher and paid unflagging attention to the text, meaning and moral content of the lessons. But I disliked the arithmetic class. I used to choose a seat at the back during this period. The arithmetic teacher matched his dreaded subject in appearance; the vertical white-red-white caste mark on his forehead gave him a permanent frown. I could not help thinking that he resembled a tiger cub I had seen in the zoo.

One day I was listening to the drone of his voice without paying attention to what he was saying. He had covered the blackboard with numbers, along with several plus, minus and equal signs and multiplication and division symbols. He had asked us to copy down the whole problem and solve it. The class was busy tackling it and so was I, supposedly. I could not make head or tail of it but I pretended to be engaged in the task too. Actually I was doodling and sketching figures in the margin of my exercise book!

Silence reigned except for the rustle of paper, clearing of throats and an occasional thump of the cane on the table as the teacher asserted his presence. He was prowling quietly between the desks, inspecting our work.

Suddenly I felt a piercing pain in my left ear. The teacher was twisting it and at the same time pulling me up by it! 'You rascal,' he shouted, 'making fun of me! You will answer for this mischief!' 'Where have I made fun of you, sir!' I moaned. 'Here!' he shouted shoving the exercise book in my face and pointing to a creature like a tiger cub I had drawn. He slapped my cheek and asked in a dangerous low tone, 'Who is it you are making fun of, if it is not me?'

Somehow the crisis subsided after arguments on both sides, with the teacher insisting it was his distorted image while I pleaded in tears that it was only a harmless doodle of a tiger cub.

It was no doubt a very unpleasant incident. But many years later I realized, as I matured in my profession, that the confrontation with the teacher was indeed beneficial. It was a moment of discovery vital to my understanding of the art of caricature. Behind the mask of the teacher's public face, a person like a tiger cub could be discerned. There were other teachers whose looks could be associated with those of animals and birds. An active imagination, fuelled by a keen sense of absurdity, could even see the human resemblance to inanimate objects such as old buildings, the shape of bottles in a drugstore, or to certain models of automobiles.

This observation would certainly seem crazy to those with normal vision and thinking habits. A cartoonist born with a cock-eyed vision manipulates a face or a human situation and distorts it without losing the essence of humour.

*

The English language was not taught to us till we neared the first year of lower secondary. Even then it was the alphabet and simple words like apple, cat, book, cap, at an age when we ought to have been able to manage complete sentences.

It was embarrassing when my sisters and their children came from Madras to escape the summer heat. These relatives were highly sophisticated in their behaviour and always conversed in stylish convent-school English. With my Kannada municipal primary school background I felt like an unlettered rustic among them. I made up for it with supercilious behaviour and snide remarks about them. I was squarely slapped on the cheek, making the situation still worse. But during their prolonged summer sojourn with us their superior airs wore off and by and by we became acceptable to each other as companions and playmates.

When the time for their departure came it broke my heart. A sense of desolation enveloped me. I hated the sight of labelled trunks, suitcases, baskets of fruit and hold-alls piled up in the veranda to be carted away in a tonga to the railway station, followed by another one carrying sisters, nephews and nieces. (Later in life I married one of the nieces, Kamala.) But I was resilient. My sense of emptiness after the guests had left did not last long, thanks to my houseful of brothers. For most of the day, some of us were always chatting, whistling, laughing or singing. All, of course, out of earshot of Father who sat far away in his room on a commodious sofa, reading a book as always.

I spent more time with my brothers Balaram and Ramachandran, because we were close in age. Balaram was fond of working with his hands, shaping pieces of wood or making aeroplanes with wire and paper. He had built a real telescope with magnifying glasses and discarded spectacles. This gave us a closer view of the Chamundi temple on the hill some ten kilometres from our kitchen window. We could actually see the devotees climbing up and down the steps of the temple. Balaram was adept at carpentry, and repaired damaged furniture, shaped cricket bats for us and even made a jewellery box for my mother, complete with red velvet lining. But he had inherited our father's quick temper. He could not tolerate me biting my fingernails, breathing heavily or clearing my throat if I was standing close to him and watching him work.

Not so Ramachandran, alias Dubbu. He was an outdoor creature. He was an expert at climbing the various trees in our vast compound and racing along the top of the compound wall enclosing our garden. He would jump off and disappear at the sight of an elder appearing on the scene.

I used to imitate all his antics, but not always with success. Sometimes he himself would not allow me to try some of his tricks because he feared I would break my neck and get him into trouble.

However, he taught me to climb a huge mango tree in the garden. We practically lived in it during the mango season. We used to climb up and sit on our favourite branches and eat quantities of raw mangoes garnished with the salt and chilli powder we carried with us. Whenever I had an accident while climbing, or if I bruised myself, the innovative Dubbu immediately applied mud to the wound and rubbed it in for a quick cure. He also flung a couple of raw mangoes in the direction of the Chamundi hill as a grateful offering to the goddess for saving me from more serious injury. He did not bother about the neighbours' windows and tiled roofs which were in the flight path of the mangoes.

Dubbu was highly imaginative and narrated stories of ghosts, demons and wild animals with such vividness that I listened to him in horrified fascination and had nightmares at night. He told me that underneath every rock and stone in the garden there were tiny people living in houses with cars, animals and so on. But these creatures disappeared the moment the stone was lifted. His tales were so convincing that I almost glimpsed these denizens peeping out from under the rocks.

Dubbu had an unused old thick diary in which he drew pictures of animals, people and birds, with a running commentary. He drew sequences of creatures in the corners of the pages; when he flicked them rapidly he created the illusion of birds flapping their wings and men moving their limbs.

Thus he was engaged busily in inventing and discovering something or the other all the time. There was never a dull moment in his company, but between us tension frequently cropped up over matters of not carrying out his orders. He suspected that I had been telling the household of his secret experiments with fire in the kitchen and with the cauldron of water in the bathroom or his habit of eating raw rice and pulses taken from the store room and so on. When he was convinced I deserved to be thrashed, he set about it mindlessly, till Mother heard my howling and rescued me, ordering me to stay away from him.

But after my crying died down and tears dried up, I become bored and went looking for him in all possible hiding places; the garage, the room where we stored wood, the loft and the treetops. Equally bored perhaps, he revealed himself in one of these places. As if we had never fought, we began to keep company again.

One day Dubbu returned from school with a high fever. He was bedridden with typhoid for several months. He finally emerged from the ordeals of fever, delirium, physical weakness, slow recovery and convalescence, and resumed his normal activities. But he was a changed person now. Much of his wild restless spirit had become subdued. He was hardly seen climbing trees or running around in the garden in the midday sun.

Once in a while, during vacations when our sisters and their children were not visiting us, Mother took her younger three sons to Madras for a change. We stayed with our grandmother, who presided over a huge family consisting of several grandchildren.

The most exciting part of going to Madras was the train journey. All three of us sat in a row glued to the windows, mesmerized by the panorama of the moving landscape—huts, villages, level crossings, clusters of trees, distant hills, flocks of sheep, a lone wayfarer on the horizon with a load on his head, emerald-green paddy fields, etc. I was fascinated by the rhythmic rise and fall of the telegraph wires in synchrony with the rushing clatter of the train's wheels. But when we approached a station or sighted a cow on the track, the engine hooted and billowed black smoke. Coal dust stung our eyes. For the rest of the journey we stared at the passing landscape with red, smarting eyes.

Madras at that time of the year was as hot as an oven. Morning, noon and night, the temperature remained the same. The ceiling fans wafted hot air but they were used mostly to keep the mosquitoes and flies at bay.

My elder uncle was both a Tamil and an English scholar. He brought out a Tamil periodical much admired by the literary circles. He had a philosophic temperament—gentle, forgiving and humorous.

The younger uncle was a car salesman. He drove vehicles at top speed, drank heavily and smoked excessively. It was said he never failed to sell a car, even if the party was disinclined to buy one. He even sold quite a few cars to the Maharaja of Mysore, who was supposed to be quite unapproachable by anyone except his inner circle of courtiers.

My uncle was known for his courage in the face of all odds, to the point of endangering his life. Once he drove down from the Nilgiri hills to Mysore in a car without brakes by skilfully manipulating the gears. Another time he was supposed to have outwitted some highway robbers at the dead of night when his car was waylaid on the Bangalore-Mysore road. When the dacoits stood across the road he pretended to stop, and when the marauders came closer he accelerated the car and scooted off at a terrific speed!

There were quite a few cousins of my age in the vast sprawling house, but they all seemed to belong to another culture altogether—not quite compatible with the polished breed we from Mysore considered ourselves to be. None of them wore a shirt. They were clad only in dhotis, even when they went out. They washed and bathed under the garden tap in the open any number of times in a day, whenever they felt like it, unquestioned by the elders. The huge house had a courtyard, tall pillars, staircases and innumerable rooms. The heavy carved doors had brass knobs. My cousins seemed to be all over the house all the time, screaming, playing and jumping about till late at night. They lay down wherever they were when sleep overcame them. Their strange habits bothered me. I began to plead with my mother to take me back to Mysore.

Particularly depressing was the sight of constant funeral processions in the street, on the way to the nearby graveyard as well as the cremation ground. I suffered greatly at night on this account, even though I was lying close to my mother. It was harrowing to hear the approaching drums, followed by the gaslit procession escorting the corpse. Eerie silhouettes of the mourners were thrown across our wall. Seized with dread, I huddled close to Mother and cried.

I felt the day of deliverance had come when we departed for Mysore!

*

Till now we had only a rudimentary knowledge of English. But when we entered the first year of middle school the teaching of English suddenly began in the right royal manner.

Suddenly from 'B for Bat' and 'C for Cat' we were thrust into the erudite company of Addison and Steele, Goldsmith and Chesterton. All other subjects also began to be taught in English. Kannada was relegated to the status of a second language. I managed, since I came from a home with a background of literary interests and fondness for English. My brothers conversed in English mixed with Tamil or Kannada. Moods of anger or humour were expressed in English along with Tamil or Kannada. So also news of happenings in the world and college gossip. They seemed unaware of the language they spoke. But any mistake in grammar was immediately frowned upon and corrected. To get poor marks in English was considered a sign of low mental calibre, and foretold gloomy future prospects. But weakness in any of the other subjects—history, geography, hygiene—was condoned.

Quite a few of my classmates found it difficult to learn English. Most of them were first-generation learners, both in Kannada and English. For them to read and understand an essay by Addison written centuries ago on Sir Roger Coverley, a royal peer of those days, was impossible. The piece contained unmanageable sentences, unpronounceable names and understated, very British humour. There was another essay, entitled 'Steeplechase', in the same textbook written by some celebrated writer. It was so incomprehensible to the poor teacher that he did not venture to teach it. He quietly skipped it, saying that it was not important. Some of the masters who conducted the English classes were ill-qualified to teach the language to their totally ignorant pupils. Once during the translation class, when we had to translate English into Kannada and vice versa, the sentence in question was: 'We had a picnic under a tree in the park.' 'What is picnic, sir?' a boy asked. The teacher pondered over the question for endless minutes. Finally he replied, 'Picnic? Well, it's a kind of fruit. They all sat and ate that from the tree.' Finding themselves unequal to face the sudden onslaught of English, many abandoned education and joined the unlettered masses of the subcontinent.

If I had any difficulty in understanding a piece of poetry or in writing an essay I had an advantage over most others in my class. Any of my well informed and knowledgeable brothers could have helped me out. But it was risky. Somehow such consultations always strayed away from the issue under consideration and I would be questioned about other subjects, my proficiency in geometry, geography or Kannada. My strengths and weaknesses in these were rigorously tested, often resulting in tears and humiliation.

I did not know at that time that among my brothers was a great Indian writer in English in the making, R.K. Narayan! If he happened to help me, I of course benefited immensely. But Narayan did not bother with my academic problems. He turned his attention to my personal appearance and habits. He would say that my hair was a bit too wild and could do with a trim, a little oil and combing, and that I should give up biting my nails (although he nibbled at his even while reprimanding me), and that my shirt front was not a towel meant for wiping my hands, mouth and face.

Of all my brothers, somehow Narayan appointed himself as my mentor and kept a watch on me as I climbed trees, learnt to ride a bicycle and played cricket inside our compound. All of these activities were strictly prohibited. I was part of a cricketing gang I named the Rough And Tough And Jolly Team. We wandered about in the streets and bylanes looking for a patch of ground on which to play.

Once I found a compact little field where I established my cricket club, and from then on our team flourished as the most formidable challenger in the locality. But the opponents were always there, a nameless itinerant group encroaching on our turf.

One day when a match was in full swing, an old lady walked straight into the middle of the pitch and ordered us to get out immediately. We were stunned. All the players looked at me for the next move as I was captain of the Rough and Tough and Jolly Team. 'Why should we?' I demanded. 'Because this plot of ground belongs to us and we pay taxes on it and you have no right to play here. Now get out!' I shouted back, 'No, this land belongs to my uncle!' having heard vaguely that some distant relative had claims over it. 'Nonsense! Get out before I call the police!' she screamed, pulling out the stumps and throwing them in all directions. We had no way to establish our claim. We left, shouting that we would be back. Narayan wrote a story called 'The Rega Cricket Club' based on this frustrating incident.

Some years earlier Narayan had written another story inspired by my activity. It was called 'Dodu the Money Maker'. It was about a little fellow who badly needed money to buy peanuts. This story won him an award in a literary competition sponsored by a magazine in Madras.

I looked upon the business of sitting daily in a classroom for hours, to study, learn and face examinations, as an unavoidable family and social obligation. But I believed drawing and sketching were vital commitments to my whole future life. Even when memorizing the year of Ashoka's Kalinga war or the number of zones the earth was divided into, or the nature of verb, gender and noun, I turned to the blank flyleaves that each textbook graciously provided, and filled them profusely with sketches to reduce the strain of classroom learning. I drew objects that caught my eye outside the window of my room—the dry twigs, leaves, the lizard-like creature crawling about, the servant chopping firewood and, of course, any number of crows in various postures on the rooftops of the buildings opposite. Relaxed thus, I used to get back to my studies refreshed. As a result not a square inch of space was left untouched by my restless pencil, in any of my textbooks.

At this period of my life I was not yet old enough to browse through the newspapers which everyone at home was passing from hand to hand and reading with great concentration. One day, by accident, I saw a cartoon opposite the editorial page of the *Hindu*. I studied it. It made no sense to me, but the brilliance of its draftmanship was stunning and held my attention for a long time. The cartoon showed three figures in a boat in a stormy sea with waves rising like mountains. The giant waves, the boat, the people were all labelled. I looked at the name of this marvellous artist at the bottom of the cartoon. It was brief and bold and I read it as 'cow'.

From that day on I looked for the 'cow' cartoon which appeared now and then in the *Hindu*. I spent hours gazing at the drawing and observing its finer points; the gentle caricature of faces, the effortless flow of lines, the perspective, the drapery—all done in controlled distortion—a masterpiece of visual satire. But of course I understood nothing of the cartoon's political content. With great effort I tried to grasp that too. All that I could read was words written on the figures such as, 'Armament', 'Trade Wars', 'League of Nations', and so on. I became an avid follower of this illustrator's work. Only much later I learnt his name was not 'cow' but 'LOW'—the world-renowned Sir David Low. As I grew up I gathered scraps of information about him. I learnt he was an immigrant from New Zealand settled in London working for the *Evening Standard* as its political cartoonist. In course of time I knew everything about him, that he had a dog called Spotty, that he had two daughters, that he went to a movie every day but got out before the show ended for he found that more interesting and so on. I had also collected quite a few books containing his political cartoons and caricatures.

The strangest moment of my life occurred one morning in 1952. By then I had already worked five years with the *Times of India* as its political cartoonist. I always went to the office at 8.30 in the morning before anyone had arrived. That day as I entered my room I was astonished to see a couple sitting in the chairs opposite my desk. It was Mr and Mrs David Low. This was the man I had dreamt of seeing somewhere, sometime one day without much hope since childhood. Certainly not so casually right in my own room that morning!

After the initial shock, the wonder and disbelief alternating inside me like blinking lights subsided. I gathered my wits and talked to my visitors with a strange continuity, perhaps as a result of years of familiarity with Low's life and work. I asked if he was on one of his trips to Hong Kong. I had read somewhere that one of his daughters was married to a businessman there and Low visited them regularly every three years. His ship had docked that day at Bombay for a few hours. They had enough time get off the ship and take a walk down Ballard Pier. Somehow they found themselves near the *Times of India* building, and finally they wound up in my room, guided by a passing night-shift reporter on his way home.

I took the couple on a sightseeing trip which concluded with a view from the Malabar Hill. Here I experienced my most embarrassing moment. Marive Drive looked enchanting—the sea, the skyline, Chowpatty beach. I could see the Lows were very impressed with the landscape. I looked on proudly, as if it was all my creation. The tranquil silence, chirping birds, fragrant flowers, the salubrious air, all went to my head. I broke the silence, boasting, 'So, Mr Low, most foreign visitors come to India looking for sadhus, snake charmers, elephants and tigers. I hope you have gathered a different impression of our country to take home.' I swept my hand dramatically at the entire panorama. At that very instance I thought I heard a faint musical note. It increased in volume. We could tell it was unmistakably emanating from a wind instrument. It was soon followed by a snake charmer. He had made himself resemble the Hollywood idea of an Indian snake charmer. I was greatly embarrassed by the sudden appearance of this fellow on the scene. Low directed all his attention with a bemused expression that was so eloquent on the snake and its charmer. The master of subtle satire did not have to turn round to look at me to rub in the fact what a ridiculous situation I had jockeyed myself into. I took refuge in a loud guffaw and said gallantly, 'Let us go before the rope-trick fellow, the sadhu, the elephants and tigers follow, Mr Low.'

*

The ups and downs of my life consisted of trivial events. The gift of a cricket bat from a visiting sister, or some unexpected cash slipped into my pocket by a generous brother so that I could go to a movie or buy a masala dosa at Anand Bhavan made me immensely happy. The younger of the two sisters, who became my mother-in-law later in life, even presented me with a bicycle!

But all these did not help. If I faced defeat in a cricket or football match, or had an argument with Mother over taking an oil bath, or if I fought with a brother for some reason, I used to go about enveloped in gloom. Only when something good occurred would my spirits be elevated and the depression wiped out.

My longest period of emotional suffering came about when my best friend HK disillusioned me by his unexpected odd behaviour. We had both entered the 'A' class as infants on the same day, coincidentally the same day the free Municipal Primary school started, and sat together on the same bench. We sat together that way throughout our educational career till we passed out of college clutching a BA degree each years later.

At the time I was the captain of the Rough and Tough and Jolly Team, HK was the vice captain and a very important member of our group. He was a good bowler as well as an able batsman. Our interests and opinions usually coincided on all matters, and there was not a day of tension or misunderstanding. He always tended to take the line of least resistance. But then he, my soulmate, began to act in a strange manner. He suddenly ignored the Rough and Tough and Jolly Team. He never showed up at the field at the weekend matches, and vanished. Later I came to learn that he was cycling round the streets of Mysore with a chap called Sheriff! They were seen at Anand Bhavan, the eating house and also at the movies and city parks. It really broke my heart to see a trusted friend betray me thus for no apparent reason.

Disillusionment and frustration at this cruel letdown plunged me in gloom which became apparent to everyone around. With a captain who had lost interest in cricket matches the Rough and Tough and Jolly Team gradually disintegrated and disappeared.

I wandered around desolate and companionless for some time. Then one day I went looking for HK and found him on the Kukanhalikeve tank bund, a favourite spot for walks and contemplation, in the company of Sheriff, of course. I joined them as if nothing had happened between us! As far as they were concerned, indeed apparently nothing had happened. From then on I went along with them in their jaunts and we formed a happy trio.

Life once again resumed its even tenor. We discovered new diversions and adventures and carried on merrily.

But soon I was to experience the shock that transformed me from a child into an adult. My father went out with a friend in his car, as was part of his normal daily routine. Later that evening the car returned and two people got out, supporting Father on either side and trying to bring him to the house. He had had a paralytic stroke in the car while returning from Krishnaraja Sagara, a dam across the river Kaveri. It was a tourist spot about fourteen kilometres from Mysore. From that day on the pattern of our entire household changed. The main concern of everyone was Father and his requirements. Each one of us lent a hand in taking care of him, feeding him, bathing him, and putting him to bed, since he was totally immobilized.

As days went by we got used to the routine, and he too showed signs of improvement. He began to walk a little, holding on to a helping hand or a walking stick. But there were sudden recurrent setbacks in his progress and I would be asked to rush off on my bicycle to call Dr Krishna Rao, who had once been father's student. He would come to examine Father, joke a little, prescribe medicines and assure Mother and the anxious circle of servants and sons that Father would be all right in the morning and leave behind renewed hope and cheer and depart.

In a year or so Father did recover sufficiently and began to insist he be shifted to his spacious room upstairs, where he had his books in the revolving shelf, his table, chair and bed. My mother thought it was a good idea. For nearly a year Father had been occupying the main hall where he had been settled following the stroke. His presence there inhibited the normal household activities. The usual domestic noises and smells from the kitchen and the loud voices of visitors annoyed Father. So he was gently escorted to his own private room. He settled down comfortably there and even moved about on his own. I got used to Father's semi-invalid state. I went back to my routine and went to school, played with friends, sat in HK's room at his house and sketched whatever I saw through the window.

Mother rarely went to the club now, having to take care of Father. She engaged herself reading magazines and books. She was also an expert on decorating and dressing colour prints of gods and goddesses. She had even won a silver medal and a citation at the Mysore Dussehra Exhibition for her handiwork. Now she devoted more time to it and produced gorgeous looking gods in purple velvet coats, silk dhotis with gold thread, embellishments and artificial diamond crowns and jewellery.

But the precarious calm did not last long. One morning pandemonium erupted. I saw the servant and cook running upstairs two steps at a time. Mother was shouting for help from the corridor upstairs. My elder brother was rushing towards Father's room. The others were running in all directions, shouting orders. I could not make out what was really happening. Finally I gathered that Father had collapsed in the bathroom and that the door was bolted from inside. I ran at once to the open terrace, vaulted over the short wall and slid on to the catwalk which circled the entire sprawling bungalow and passed under Father's bathroom window. I moved on the one-foot ledge like a tightrope walker without any support and a fifty-foot sheer plunge below. By the time I reached the window my brothers had come to know what I was up to. They had rushed to the garden to watch me with anxiety. Voices rose from below counselling caution and telling me that I was a reckless fool! Through the crossbars of the window I saw the sad sight of Father sprawled on the floor helplessly. I turned to the crowd below and asked for a bamboo pole. Somebody threw one up, fortunately without asking questions.

With one hand I firmly held on to the window bar and with the help of the pole I reached for the bolt of the bathroom door. With a couple of firm taps, I finally succeeded in releasing the latch. The group below watched me with bated breath. The moment they got the signal that I had done the job, they rushed into the house to attend to Father.

Then I worked my way carefully along the catwalk to safety. Father had suffered a haemorrhage of the brain. He lost the power of speech, sight and movement. A couple of months later he mercifully passed away.

It took the household some time to adjust to the absence of Father, who was at that time the only breadwinner. He left behind no debts or liabilities, nor did he bequeath us any property.

He did not believe in having any immovable

possessions. Even as a newly-married young man, he had surrendered to his elder brother a chilli plantation which he had legally inherited. He thought it was too much trouble supervising and maintaining it. He felt it would interfere with his scholarly pursuits, and that his elder brother was inherently better suited to the job because of his rustic temperament.

Encouraged by Father's indifference to property, this brother had planned to make certain conventional moves to usurp the holding without actually seeming to do so. But before even the first step was taken towards this end, Father handed over his entire share of the plantation and everything that went with it to the astonished brother on a platter, packed his bags and departed permanently for Mysore.

Although Father was not a socializing man and would spend all his time in his room reading, after his death I felt his absence at home keenly. His coat-stand, wardrobe, the several pairs of shoes he had ordered from London and the collection of various types of walking sticks were all a painful reminder of him. The elders at home were busy and preoccupied with the task of coping with our financial difficulties, but the pattern of my own life was unchanged—going to school, the company of HK in the evenings, studying, appearing for the exams and moving on from class to class.

Then one day I found myself promoted to the high school. Here, apart from the usual subjects such as history, geography, science and mathematics, I had to choose an optional subject for specialization: botany, chemistry and so on. Luckily the list included drawing and painting. Since the elders at home were not in the habit of interfering with whatever I did, as long as it was within reason, I naturally chose this for my optional.

The general classes contained about fifty students. But our drawing class which met twice a week had only five boys. This subject was looked upon something fit only for predetermined high school drop-outs. In keeping with this notion my colleagues were shabbily dressed, unkempt dull fellows who could neither draw nor paint.

Our drawing teacher was a Maharashtrian, a product of the prestigious JJ School of Arts. He was always dressed in an immaculate off-white silk suit including a waistcoat and a tie. He crowned it all with red headgear with gold dangling tassels—like those worn by freedom fighters from Maharashtra. His complexion was very fair, one could almost see the blood coursing under translucent skin. He smelt of the scented supari he munched all the time.

On the first day he set a wooden cube about two feet square on a stool in front of us, to teach us the rules of perspective and the illusion of parallel lines meeting at infinity. Next he taught us to measure the length and depth of an object with the help of a pencil held at arm's length viewing the object in relation to it with one eye shut. Then he asked us to draw the cube.

As I had guessed, I was the only one who could draw it correctly. I had already learnt without the help of a teacher the technique of drawing a cube. The buildings, streets, tables and chairs I used to sketch were basically all cubes. The teacher controlled his surprise at my efforts and exempted me from bothering about some of the more rudimentary lessons he had to teach the others.

At about this time I got into the company of some of

the better known professional painters of Mysore, through a painter of water colours who was a friend of one of my brothers.

I became friendly with the artists and got to know their work, which was strictly formal and academic. They bore titles such as *Love*, depicting a pretty girl with rosy cheeks reclining on a pillow while anxious parents proferred fruit, milk and jewellery; or *Reverie*, again a damsel draped in heavy ornaments resting on a purple bolster and gazing heavenward, lost in thought; or *Companion*, showing an averagely pretty girl staring at a caged parrot. These creations belonged to the artists' imagination heavily influenced by the European paintings of the seventeenth and eighteenth centuries. Since there were not many takers for such work, the artists eked out a living by painting portraits of the society big-wigs, rich merchants who had done philanthrophic work or people connected with royalty. These portraits were meant to be hung in public buildings.

The Maharaja of Mysore came to the rescue of these artists, who were wandering about like lost sheep and aimlessly waiting for an occasional commission for a portrait.

His Highness ordered an enormous mural for his palace. The subject was the famous Dussehra procession. The painting was to depict the entire scene, from the arched gates of the palace where the procession started to the termination point called Banni Mantap about ten miles away. The Maharaja was to be shown sitting on the caprisoned royal elephant in his golden howda, followed by his entire entourage consisting of elephants, carriages, important officials on horseback, cavalry regiments, a camel brigade and foot soldiers, besides the general crowd watching from rooftops, windows and balconies. It was a mammoth job. An old palace fully equipped with stretched canvases, easels, paints and brushes was alotted as the studio for this project.

All the painters foregathered cheerfully every day in the vast hall of the studio, greeting each other, laughing, chatting and painting the procession. I became a regular visitor to this place and enjoyed the company of the artists, who were simple-minded and uncomplicated. When their panel was finished, it was to adorn one entire side of the hall of the main palace.

Once in a while during holidays the landscape artist and I used to get on our bicycles with our equipment and pedal away to some place outside the town to look for subjects to paint.

In this respect Mysore was a landscape painter's dream—enchanting rock formations at the foothills of Chamundi; gigantic banyan trees, ancient, nameless, dateless ruins overgrown with shrubs and weeds as if artificially arranged; lakes, huts, village roads. We chose one of these as a subject, sat on our folding stools and painted till the sun touched the western horizon with blazing orange. In between we had an hour's break to have our packed lunch and discuss the finer points of the tree or the ruin we were engaged in capturing on the paper in watercolour. By the time we turned back home we were fatigued but contented with a sense of fulfilment.

One day Vasu, an artist engaged to fill in the minor details of the Dussehra mural in the Palace Studio, overheard us planning the usual painting excursion. He was eager to join us, promising to show us some exotic haunts ideal for painting, which we could never have seen before.

I got up very early on the appointed day and called on my friend. Vasu was to join us later. The two of us went to the nearby Udipi hotel and ate our breakfast, which included nearly every item on the menu: masala dosa, idli, methuwada, uppuma and coffee. We did not order any packed lunch as we used to, because Vasu insisted he should be allowed to take care of that.

On the deserted Mysore-Ooty Trunk Road we sat on a culvert and waited for Vasu. We soon sighted him at a distance on the deserted road, pedalling towards us. As he neared we saw the load he carried: a portable easel, a bag with painting material slung onto the handlebar, and a canvas bag containing our lunch firmly secured to the carrier.

From that point on he became our guide and led the way. He took us through narrow bylanes paved with red chillies and pulses for drying. We could hardly find a place to set our feet. Then we were taken across rice fields and tank bunds, pushing our bicycles all the way. After hours of journeying thus we arrived at the village which seemed to be Vasu's destination.

There was a well in the shade of a gigantic margosa tree. Dilapidated huts were overgrown with grass and wild plants. A broken cart wheel rested against a fence, completing a perfect composition. Commenting on such subtleties, we began to move around, leaving the bicycles under the margosa tree. The whole place was still and silent. There wasn't even the noise of crows. Not a soul could be seen anywhere. The doors of the huts were ajar. There was no sign that they were inhabited. We peeped into one of them. There were some broken mud pots and half-burnt faggots scattered around. Weeds and plants were pushing their way into the hut. The serpentining roots of trees outside had cracked the walls and lifted up the floor slabs and had made their entry.

There were about fifty huts in the village, all of them deserted and crumbling. We asked Vasu about the cause of such desolation and the weird state of the village. 'I am told cholera and plague had driven the people out,' he said casually. I was alarmed that the epidemic might be still lingering waiting for its prey. 'How long ago was this?' I asked. 'Oh, fifty or a hundred or two hundred years ago, I think.' He looked at his watch and said, 'It is past noon. By the time we settle down and finish our lunch it will be one o'clock. We will hardly have time for painting.' We discussed the matter and decided that we would come back another day, after all we knew the place now.

We sat down on a boulder under the shade of the margosa tree and prepared to have our lunch.

Vasu spread out sheets of old newspaper in front of us and started unpacking the lunch. He took out a dozen potatoes, a handful of ladies' fingers, assorted beans and brinjals. I was shocked to see that the vegetables were uncooked. 'These are raw. How are we to eat them?' my friend enquired. 'Eat. It is good for health. Always eat vegetables uncooked.' He launched on, expounding the virtues of uncooked vegetables and their benefits while he chewed a ladies' finger. I pushed the veritable vegetable market towards him and got up. So did my friend. 'Why? Why? Why?' Vasu asked, bewildered. We just picked up our bicycles and left. He did not make any attempt to stop us but continued to crunch the ladies' fingers. It was quite late when we reached our homes, completely fagged out and hungry.

*

One day my Kannada teacher asked me to call on a Kannada writer who was well known as a humorist. The teacher said that the writer had some interesting proposition to make. Very soon I called on him. Of course, he already knew our family and me as the illustrator of Narayan's short stories in the *Hindu*. He had also seen the special issue of the college magazine containing quite a few of my cartoons. Although I was far from entering the portals of the university, yet I was invited to illustrate the articles for the magazine. I did a cover for the issue, which depicted a melting candle shedding brilliant light on an open tome resting below it. The editors were so pleased with my drawings that they paid me a modest honorarium, mentioned their appreciation in the editorial and printed my photograph and captioned it 'Our Artist'.

I was surprised to see my photograph! I wondered how the editors could have got at it. Later I learnt of the conspiracy utilizing the services of my brother on oath of secrecy to get the photograph smuggled out of the family album.

The Kannada writer I called on had seen and appreciated all my efforts. He suggested I contribute cartoons to a new humorous magazine that was to be started in Bangalore. A practicing doctor there was planning a monthly publication and wanted five or six cartoons from me. I would be a sort of partner and would be remunerated by a share in the profits.

The magazine was called *Koravanji*. I sketched a vivacious looking damsel in the pose of a folk dancer. At that time World War II was on and its effect was felt even in

Mysore. There were blackouts at night, food rationing, shortages of essential commodities. All these yielded rich material for my funny cartoons for the new magazine. The publication also contained good reading material written by competent authors. The magazine soon picked up circulation and became a talking point among the public. I had not realized that along with *Koravanji* I too had gained some admirers among the readers, till one day a police inspector caught me. I was going about on my bicycle without renewing my licence for the vehicle. It had lapsed some months before. His assistant held the handlebar while the inspector examined the brass licence plate. Then he took out a notebook and asked my name and address. I went cold all over, pleading and bluffing that I had been ill, bed-ridden, out of town. I promised that I would get the licence renewed immediately. But he insisted on taking down my particulars. I had a momentary urge to pass on a false name and address. But I dithered and told the truth. He ordered me to report at the licencing office the next day. I hopped on my bike and was about to push off when he asked, 'Are you the *Koravanji* Laxman?' He was delighted to know that I was, shook hands with me, scrached my name and address from the offenders' list, and gave some friendly advice about getting the license without delay, and I would be exempt from paying the fine, he said.

The ten days of the Dussehra festival were celebrated with a great deal of grandeur. The whole city of Mysore was aglow at night—all the public buildings were floodlit. The centre of attraction was the palace, virtually clothed in millions of electric bulbs, and blazing like a torch.

During this season visitors from all over India and

abroad poured into Mysore. But I had only one purpose—that was the compulsory visit to the Dussehra exhibition. A vast complex of stalls and shops was built. Huge numbers of traders and manufacturers took advantage of it, coming from all over India to exhibit their goods: textiles, machinery, cosmetics, sports goods and a hundred other items. Besides there were game parlours, restaurants, magic shows and so on. The whole population of Mysore turned up at this arena in the evenings. Here one met old friends; forgotten faces were recalled; college professors and retired officials were relaxed and chummy. In the jostling crowd I ran into my own brothers with their friends again and again. Even if people had not come to buy anything, it was great fun just wandering around chatting, eating and laughing away the ten days of Dussehra.

There was also an art gallery in the exhibition ground, where works of eminent painters from Bengal, Gujarat, Maharashtra, Hyderabad and other states were displayed. These were judged by a panel of experts, and gold and silver medals, cash prizes and certificates of merit were awarded to the best work. I used to spend a good deal of time at the art gallery. I was thrilled by the variety of techniques these artists used, in water colour, oil, charcoal and pen and ink!

The following year I decided to enter my own efforts. I did caricatures of some prominent local personalities, including Sir Mirza Ismail, the Dewan of Mysore. This was the first time caricatures were admitted within the sacred precincts of the fine arts. Along with these satirical sketches I also included a few colour cartoons of people bargaining with vegetable sellers in the market place, a gypsy with a monkey, a little girl crying over a broken pot of milk, a beggar playing on a violin made from a coconut shell. I also presented a dozen pencil drawings showing my three-year-old nephew in a series of moods—playing with a ball, running, eating, sleeping, crying and so on. There was a very strict selection board and I was afraid my work would be rejected. But it was included in the exhibition, to my utter surprise. It was a great moment in my life, similar to the one many years earlier when my primary school teacher had patted me on the back, complimenting me on my drawing of a leaf! I was proud to see my cartoons exhibited along with the work of the country's veteran artists. I was even awarded a cash prize for my 'Glimpses of Thumbi', the sketches of my little nephew captured in action!

Finally the season's activities came to an end. The visitors departed to their homes, the illuminations were switched off, the hubbub and noise subsided, and silence returned to Mysore.

One evening my mother was sitting in a cane chair in the veranda, counting her prayer beads. She would be in a meditative mood counting crystal prayer beads at that moment. I sat on the step next to her chair. Peering into the night and at the outline of the trees in the garden, I listened to the drone of insects in the bushes. Suddenly I heard the hooves of a horse in the dark street. A few minutes later the gate made the usual long-drawn-out squeak and sound of boots on the gravel path approached. A cavalryman in full regalia stood in front of us and handed over a letter, stood at attention, saluted, withdrew and galloped away. I thought the letter was for my brother Srinivasan who worked in the palace secretariat. But I was surprised to see that the letter bore my name.

It was from Sir Charles Todhunter, one of the senior advisers to His Highness. I could not make head or tail of the letter. My mother and my two brothers Balaram and Dubbu who had joined us examined the mysterious letter and differed on the meaning of its contents. It read.

> Rao wrote on the note I had put up that you were none other than the brother of Srinivasan. In view of this I thought it would not be a bad idea to utilise your services for the new K.G. School being planned. Kindly see me on Thursday at 10 a.m. in my office.

So on the appointed day I applied a lot of oil to my hair and combed it back to prevent it from springing forward and covering my forehead. Then I put on a coat reserved for special occasions and got ready to see Sir Charles. My brother Srinivasan accompanied me to the office of Mr Rao, who conducted me to Sir Charles's room. He was sitting on a swivel chair before a table with his back to the entrance. He was huge, with many folds like rows of sausages on the neck. On the wall, framed in gold, hung a full-length portrait of His Highness the Maharaja wearing a pearl necklace and a blue satin robe, with feathers in his turban. There were also paintings of His Majesty the King of England; and pictures of horses standing in a field of green grass. A wall-to-wall Persian carpet covered the floor. Though there was bright sunlight outside, all the lights were on and the crystals in the chandeliers twinkled like stars.

Rao halted at a respectable distance and cleared his throat to announce our arrival. Sir Charles cleared his to acknowledge our presence, but continued with his work, whatever it was. Then suddenly he swung round and faced us.

Rao mumbled something. Sir Charles smiled and at once started talking to me so fast I could not understand a word! But Rao went on intoning, 'Yes sir, yes sir, I understand, sir. I will tell him so, sir . . .' In a few minutes the meeting was over and Sir Charles swivelled round and displayed his broad back once again.

Rao explained to me later in his room what was it all about. Lady Todhunter was in charge of a new kindergarten school for the children of the rich. I was expected to paint murals in the interior of the building to amuse, teach and generally keep the children happy!

The task seemed formidable, involving ladders,

labourers, assistants and so on. Besides, there was a chance of Lady Todhunter arriving at the work spot unannounced to inspect, give suggestions and make corrections.

Helped by my elders at home I drafted a letter addressed to Rao, saying I was still a student and had to study, attend classes, prepare for examinations; therefore I would not have time to take up this job, and should be kindly excused. In this manner I escaped the clutches of His Lordship without much difficulty.

So I thought! But a few weeks later he wanted me to design some postcards to help the war effort. Fortunately he had thought of the ideas and sent them over to me. They were pretty simple. He wanted a drawing of an Italian soldier of the most elite regiment, in a highly ornate uniform with brass buttons with gold bands and tassels. Next to the soldier I was to draw an unshaven Italian prisoner-of-war with sunken eyes and protruding cheekbones, standing behind barbed wire. The caption read: 'Join the Italian Army and See Mysore!' At that time one of the prisoner-of-war camps was located in Mysore. The second postcard was to depict the superiority of the RAF Spitfire over the German Messerschmidt. These two aircraft were to be shown chasing each other, till finally the German fighter was vanquished in a dogfight. The backdrop was to be a huge letter V (for Victory). My drawings were printed and sold as postcards. I was presented with two defence bonds of ten rupees each, whose maturity was ten years following the date of issue!

After the brief interlude with Sir Charles Todhunter, I fell into my daily routine at school and at home. Life resumed its even rhythms.

At home all of us used to gather together only at night

after dinner, lolling lazily round my mother's bed and chatting about the happenings of the day.

The latecomer to this session was Srinivasan. And still later came our eldest brother Pattabhi. Srinivasan was usually held up at the office for some reason or other concerning His Highness's tour, or arrangements for a visiting dignitary and so on. But Pattabhi arrived late because he went straight from the office to the club for a game of bridge or billiards, along with a couple of mugs of beer, his favourite drink. Finally when he did appear at the door Mother routinely asked, for as long as I could remember, 'Why so late? Go eat first and come. What will happen to your health if you eat so late?' To which, of course, no reply was expected.

All of us relaxed during the gossip hour at home. We recounted the events of the day, the people we met, the eccentricities of schoolteachers or the tyranny of bosses. Sometimes these hilarious verbal caricatures and appropriate mimicry went on till well past midnight.

By the time I got up in the morning, bathed and had my breakfast, there would be just enough time to reach the school by the first bell.

The classes were dull. The teachers were standard specimens that one found in any school in the world. I spent most of my time caricaturing them, half listening to their lectures. I was confident I would get enough marks to pass even without paying attention or taking notes. There were always studious boys in the front row who took profuse notes, and I always borrowed these at the approach of exams or tests.

One redeeming feature of school life was the history period. As an experiment the board of education temporarily introduced what was called world history, dispensing with the usual versions of Indian, European or British history. The idea was to enlighten young people about the world's great personalities—Socrates, Plato, Lenin, Mahatma Gandhi and Sun Yat-sen. No textbook existed for this course, and the teacher had to cull from various sources, make notes and then instruct the class.

I found history in this form much more enjoyable than reading it chronologically from era to era. According to classroom rumours there was another advantage in this. We believed that the answer papers would be more generously examined as the subject was at an experimental stage.

When the class concluded for the day I used to dash home at breakneck speed on my bicycle, throw the books on the table, wash, gulp down a cup of coffee and rush to HK's house as if to meet a long-lost friend! But actually we would have sat the whole day together in the classroom hardly an hour ago.

But the evening meetings were different. We rode on the cycle to Anand Bhavan for masala dosa and coffee. Then we headed towards the foothills of Chamundi, to the Lalitha Mahal, a palace built for the royal guests of the Mysore maharajas. We spent time there in the spacious gardens discussing books, movies, art, sports. And in the quiet of the surroundings we smoked a couple of cigarettes, emboldened by the knowledge that my elder brothers too were enjoying their puffs secretly somewhere.

I never liked the smell of cigarettes. It gave me no pleasure; in fact I found it nauseating. But just to keep up with the trend set by my brothers and schoolmates, I tried to develop the habit.

After witnessing the glorious sunset on the far horizon, with the brilliant sky like a vast canvas stretched from one end of the globe to another, we started our homeward journey. We pedalled our bicycles at a furious speed keeping our mouths open to let the wind blow away the smell of tobacco.

I continued to smoke throughout high school and college. Even after taking up the career of a cartoonist the habit persisted. But at the height of my smoking days I could manage to burn no more than ten cigarettes a day. I found it cumbersome to carry the matchbox or lighter and case and keep an anxious count of the number left in it. Besides, I could not sketch, read the papers, think or drive with a cigarette dangling from my lips. And I found the stale smell it left on my clothes, handkerchief and fingers repugnant. Smoking never became a habit with me. Finally it was the cigarettes that left me!

Apart from visiting the palace garden at the Chamundi foothills, at least once a week we went to the cinema. The Royal Opera House was our favourite. It always showed choice Hollywood films. The memory of this cinema hall goes back to my childhood days when there were only silent films.

I was taken to the Opera House to see a film called *The Kid*, the hero of which was a very mischievous six-year-old brat. I still remember the actor's name—Jackie Coogan.

My father, who was grim and conservative in all respects, and strictly disapproving of movies, somehow stumbled onto this film and was so thrilled by the pranks of little Coogan that he decided that I should see it. He made all arrangements to have me escorted to the theatre. I was equally taken in by the movie. After coming home I indulged in petty mischief, fancying myself to be the Kid Coogan. Mother had to keep a vigilant eye over me and check my movements for a long time till the imitative urge wore off.

I frequented the Opera House while growing up. In front of the theatre an hour before the commencement of the film, a man in a shirt and dhoti, a bagpipe with genuine tartan trimmings tucked under his arms, paced up and down as he squeezed out a sad Highland tune. This sideshow was to attract crowds to the theatre. The feature film would be some cowboy story of the wild west, full of galloping horses, jagged mountain passes, rugged heroes and pretty heroines. The actor who was a favourite with the crowd was called Tom Mix. And the white mare he rode was called Diamond. Together they fought the bad men who prowled in the wild terrain of Arizona dotted with giant cacti. Inside the cinema hall in the balcony a thin tall man in a tuxedo with long hair played background music on the piano, capturing the various moods of love, melancholy and danger. The tune matched the visuals. The hero finally galloped across the desert into the setting sun. When the lights came on at the end of the film, the pianist played 'God Save The King'.

Krishna & Co. Book Sellers, was another place we frequented. A visit to this shop signified a certain intellectual attainment. Being a university town, Mysore was teeming with teachers, professors, students, philosophers, thinkers, researchers and writers. All of them were voracious readers hungering for books, and they habitually gathered at Krishna & Co. whenever they had time, not only to buy books but just to hang around and chat and exchange views and opinions on worldly matters.

The bookshop for all the attraction it held for the book lovers was a deceptively small affair. The entire shop measured about twelve feet by six feet. A single bookshelf ran along the wall. It contained a few copies of *The Oxford English Dictionary,* all the volumes of the *Encyclopaedia Britannica*, the complete works of Shakespeare, Palgrave's *Golden Treasury*, Shaw's prefaces. Most of the space was empty except for a thermos flask and tiffin carrier containing the proprietor's lunch. He sat in a chair in front of a small table. The half-dozen chairs in front of him were always occupied by people who came to browse, or to buy books, or to gossip.

But Mr Krishna of Krishna & Co. was a miracle worker. If he did not have the books the customers wanted, he somehow produced them within forty-eight hours—literature, science, philosophy, history, mathematics and whatever else was needed.

This is where I first came across Penguin books, which had just made their appearance in Mysore. The orange covers in the hands of readers immediately distinguished the books as fiction. Likewise, biographies had blue covers, travelogues had purple, sociology, psychology and philosophy had turquoise blue, yellow was for games. People who read Penguin books with green covers were rated less highly in our opinion, as this colour proclaimed its readers were mostly interested in thrillers and murder mysteries. Spot the Penguin and guess the owner's aesthetic and intellectual bent—this was a game HK and I enjoyed in railway stations, parks, restaurants and other public places.

Mr Krishna had a large heart. He let us browse through any books we were interested in, from the titles his customers ordered. In this manner HK and I combed through entire volumes of the history of European art, from Renaissance to Impressionism. These volumes had been ordered by some library in Mysore. Mr Krishna was generous enough to delay the delivery till we had finished going through the six bulky volumes. I was thrilled to see the colour prints of Rembrandt, Velazquez, Titian, Rubens, El Greco, van Gogh, Degas and many other masters.

In later years, when I was travelling through Europe, I saw the originals of these in the museums and art galleries. I was so familiar with most of the paintings that I could identify them even from a considerable distance. This continually astonished Kamala, my wife, who always accompanied me.

Once in the Spanish city of Barcelona, I was leaving the twelfth-century cathedral when my attention was drawn to the facade of a building across the busy street. The surface seemed still not quite dry. Deep furrows formed odd patterns on the plaster, as if made with a blunt instrument. I was impressed with the firm, deft strokes. The crude and yet curiously interesting pattern they formed fascinated me. There was harmony and a strange appeal in the composition. I was commenting on this phenomenon to Kamala when our guide heard me and explained proudly with a beaming smile, 'That design you see, sir, is by Picasso, done with his own hand. It is a gift to the citizens of Barcelona. He was born here, you know.' I had not known the existence of it till that moment. But it was a moment for self-flattery and a revelation of my aesthetic sensibility.

HK and I continued our rounds; palace garden, Royal Opera House, Krishna & Co. But slowly the pleasant cool weather of Mysore was ending. One felt a touch of humidity in the air, heralding the approach of the months of March and April and the rains. The students were solemn and serious. The playground became prematurely deserted as the boys hurried home to study for the dreaded annual examinations at various levels of colleges and schools.

HK and I too parted company early in the evening, to face the formidable task of finding out what were the subjects we were weak in and which were the ones we had neglected and how to find notes to help us out. We settled down to a systematic and disciplined routine. But doubts welled up in our minds so often that we met frequently to clear them. Then we tried what was called joint study. But soon we gave that up as we felt we would ruin each other's chances of passing—we realized we spent more time chatting and giggling and thus wasting precious hours.

Whenever we happened to meet other classmates we would speculate about which questions might appear and which chapters could be safely skipped. At the end of it we all entered the examination hall nervous and unsure. We were appearing for the secondary school-leaving certificate examination. If we passed we would be leaving high school and entering intermediate college. After the gruelling fortnight, on the last day of the examination we rushed out of the hall screaming, shouting and smashing ink bottles on the white walls of the school. Some of the boys, more confident of passing, tore up their carefully prepared notes in a frenzy and threw them up in the air, or burnt their textbooks on the steps of the high school.

During the vacation I continued with my routine, practicing sketching, preparing cartoons for a few periodicals, and illustrating my brother Narayan's short stories for the *Hindu*. I did not worry about the announcement of examinations results as I was confident of passing. When the results were announced three months later, I had fared surprisingly well in most subjects, including science and arithmetic in which I was particularly weak. But I failed in Kannada by five marks. This disqualified me from entering intermediate college. I was declared eligible for any public service, which meant I could apply for a clerical post in a government office.

For a moment some defence mechanism inside me went into action and made me view the failure with total disbelief. Cousins and nieces who were on a short visit to our home stood in a semi-circle watching for my reaction.

Brief bursts of supressed laughter escaped me as I mumbled that it was all a horrible mistake and everything would be set right.

But I could not hold on to the brave stance for more than a few minutes. The thought that HK, my bosom friend who had sat next to me in the class from primary school onwards, had forged ahead and would be entering the intermediate college without me, was overwhelming. I finally broke down and cried unabashedly in front of everyone. It looked as if that was what the spectators had been waiting for!

Some my brothers arrived to console me one by one, telling how they had faced similar failures at various stages of their academic careers. My brother Narayan's words were the most comforting. He declared proudly that though he had failed in English in the entrance examination, he had survived the blow and had become an outstanding novelist in the English language.

Mother, who always remained unmoved by the failures or successes of her sons in the examinations, pushed aside the curious watchers and asked me to stop fussing about a trivial failure. She touched my forehead, declared that I had a slight fever and ordered me to bed.

This suited me, as I was feeling ashamed of my hysterical outburst. But ironically I had indeed developed real fever. Immediately I was put on a special diet and medications.

The temperature persisted for quite a few days. I used to turn towards the wall and remain in a state of deep sleep. But actually I was contemplating the move I was to make after I had recovered.

From wild despair I was settling down to a quiet resignation. I thought of people who had suffered greater tragedies in life than a mere temporary setback in their education. I recalled those who had suffered the death of their dear ones or had lost their worldly possessions in earthquakes and floods. I became philosophical and began to think in terms of constructive, practical ways to face the future. As a first step I decided to approach Narayanappa. He was a BA student studying in the college. He was a scholar in Kannada, and was so poor that he lived in the Anathalaya (Orphans' Hostel). He used to visit us once a week for his midday meal and dinner. He had this arrangement with seven other generous homes for his meals each day of the week in turn. This gesture towards deserving poor students was prevalent in Mysore at that time. So I decided to ask Narayanappa to coach me once a week in Kannada so I could prepare for the exam again.

Having given a direction to my immediate future, I felt

great relief. I cleared my mind of all nagging worries and despondency. I even took pleasure in gazing closely at the stains on the wall, the cracks and peeling plaster. I let my eyes create all sorts of images—a charging bull, a man's profile, a temple on top of a mountain. All of these would together resolve into a marching army of horses, and soldiers with flags and all.

By the time I had recovered from the fever the visiting relatives had mercifully left. As soon as I was able to leave the house, I met HK and told him about engaging Narayanappa to tutor me in Kannada. My friend said it was an excellent idea.

We both resumed our routine of cycling up to the Chamundi foothills, sitting on the rocks, talking, watching the sunset and pedalling back home.

One day I met Narayanappa and asked him to coach me. He was delighted and offered to come early for his meals and teach for an hour. I ran to my mother and broke the good news! She was happy of course, but asked how much he was to be paid as tuition fee.

Narayanappa looked so decent and sophisticated, it was difficult to calculate what to pay him. Each figure I arrived at seemed too little. And we could not afford to give an exorbitant amount just to suit his cultivated personality although we knew he was in dire need of money.

I was pondering over this dilemma when it suddenly struck me that any attempt to enter college was a waste of time! After all I was an artist, and a degree in history, economics or politics would be of no use to me. If at all, I should be a diploma holder in fine arts from some reputed institution. I discussed this stunning revelation with HK, who heartily agreed with me and suggested that I should apply to the famous Sir Jamshedji Jeejeebhoy School of Arts, Bombay—nothing less. To add further weight to his choice, he told me that the father of Rudyard Kipling, the famous writer, was once the dean of this prestigious institution.

But the problem was telling my elders about my decision to be a high school drop-out! Mother was bound to protest. She could not imagine any member of the family not graduating, and thereby becoming an outcast.

I did a great deal of strategic planning and moved cautiously. After a great deal of thought I decided that Narayan was the right person to be taken into confidence.

He had always been rather liberal-minded where education was concerned. He had aired anti-education views and was deeply critical of the way it was conducted and I hoped he would be my ally. When I told him, he took the news casually and said that one of his friends was returning to Bombay, and he would ask him to send the necessary application forms and brochures. To my astonishment, when Mother came to know she merely said, 'You draw so well already, what is there for you to learn?'

My joy knew no bounds when the application forms and booklets containing the details of JJ School of Arts arrived. HK and I sat together and studied the literature over and over again. There was a clause asking the applicant to submit a dozen specimen drawings along with the forms.

Both of us selected from my numerous sketch books the drawings suitable for submission. Then I re-drew them according to the required size, packed them carefully in cardboard padding and despatched them to the dean of the JJ School of Arts.

From that moment I began to wait for the reply. After the sixth day I became anxious; I calculated that it would take two days for my packet to reach Bombay, one day for the dean to go through my application and specimen work, and two days for the return journey, allowing one day of grace for postal delays.

I used to stand under a tree at the street corner and view the far end of the road, waiting for the khaki uniform of the postman to appear. This had become a nerve-racking daily habit.

Two weeks went by, and still there was no reply from the JJ School. People who had more experience of red tape, application processing and delays in despatch sections mentioned these as possible reasons for the delay. They described their own experiences, such as the bother involved in applying for ration cards, allotments in government housing schemes and so on. One elderly well-wisher even went on to narrate in detail, with no apparent relevance to my own case, the trouble he had persuading the city corporation to accept the tender he had quoted for repairing a stretch of a public road. And there were others who debated and argued about the number of days it took for the train to reach Bombay. But nobody was quite sure.

I began to spend time mentally composing a rude letter to the dean of the JJ School, pointing out what a tardy correspondent he was.

Sometimes I wondered that if I did get admission, how was I to journey to Bombay, whom was I to ask for a place to stay. For me Bombay was a remote country. All that I knew about it was through what was taught to me about it in geography and history at school. But one aspect of this city all the boys generally knew was that it had a locality called the red-light district where young damsels were kept in cages facing the street for men of loose morals to have their pick.

Then my thoughts turned to Narayanappa and the help he had offered to teach me Kannada. As days went by Narayanappa began to ask, 'When shall we begin our lessons?' Since I could not indefinitely postpone preparing for the exam, I gave him a vague date. I hoped that by then I would know one way or the other my future direction—the JJ School of Arts or the intermediate college.

One day when I had nearly given it up for lost, a battered packet arrived from the JJ School. It contained my specimen drawings with a covering letter bearing an Englishman's signature. It read to the effect that my drawings lacked 'the kind of talent to qualify for enrollment in our institution as a student. I earnestly advise you to continue your studies further . . .' This gratuitous advice was probably a response to the letter I had sent with the application, where I had emphasized that I was sacrificing a college career in order to have the opportunity to become a diploma-holder from the prestigious JJ School of Arts.

I felt there was no need for me to reveal the contents of the dean's letter to the elders at home. They seemed to have forgotten about my ambition and were preoccupied with their own business. I also felt great relief that I did not have to uproot myself and shift to Bombay, and face the bother of finding a place to stay and money to support myself.

I settled down to preparing for the Kannada examination. Eventually, thanks to Narayanappa, I graduated from high school.

Many years later I came to Bombay and joined the

Times of India as its political cartoonist. Ironically the newspaper offices were situated almost next to the JJ School of Arts, which I could see from my window. My cartoons appeared on the front page of the paper. They became a regular feature and people began to appreciate my satirical comments on the political events of the day.

One day as I was preparing for my day's work and thinking about a subject for a cartoon, the dean of the JJ School telephoned to say he wished to call on me. I gave him the date and time and he and his colleague dropped into my room. They both expressed admiration for my work and said they could think of no better person to distribute prizes to the winners of the annual exhibition of paintings by the students.

I gladly accepted the honour. On the appointed day the dean came to formally escort me to the auditorium. The hall was packed with students and teachers. I was taken around to view the prize-winning paintings. I made appreciative comments to those who were ambling along with me. Then we climbed on to the dais and I was shown to my seat. The faculty arranged itself on either side of me.

The dean paid glorious tributes to me as a graphic satirist, praised the quality of my draftsmanship, the masterly strokes in my cartoons, the power of caricature and so on and so forth.

I was overwhelmed by the irony of the situation. At that moment it was impossible for me to suppress the thought that the occasion could not be more ridiculous and laughable. Many years ago the dean of those times had seen no talent in me and had rejected my application for admission to the very institution where today I was being treated as an honoured guest and glorious tributes were being paid to my work. After his speech the dean requested me to distribute the prizes, silver cups, medals and certificates, which I did with a suitable smile and words of encouragement to each recipient. When I was about to resume my seat I heard whispers, 'Speech, Speech'.

I took the mike and made a brief speech, which was irresistibly a little sarcastic, almost caddish, and embarrassing to the dean and his staff. I said I was grateful to the dean who had administered the JJ School years ago for rejecting my application. If I had been accepted and had I graduated clutching a diploma in art, perhaps I would not have been the cartoonist that I had become; I would have most likely been languishing in some corner of an advertising agency, drawing visuals for mosquito repellants or pretty faces for ladies' cosmetics, or chubby babies to promote vitamin foods, perhaps bearing the name 'Crunchy, munchy Vita biscuits'.

*

I entered the junior intermediate college with the usual excitement of obtaining the leaving certificate from the high school, filling out the application form for the college, discussing and debating over the subject to be taken.

After I was given admission I thoroughly enjoyed the atmosphere of the classrooms. I liked Greek history and Roman history. New vistas were opened to me as I learned logic and psychology. We had English professors bearing names such as Rollo, MacIntosh, Eagleton. They taught us Shakespeare: *Macbeth* and *The Merchant of Venice*, but their accent and pronunciation took some time for us to get used to. Even Kannada prose and poetry were enjoyable, thanks to proficient scholars who know both Kannada and English.

I passed from the junior to senior intermediate without any difficulty. The whole college routine became relaxed and pleasant. I even started to play tennis, encouraged by my good friend HK. He was now a year senior to me in college but we resumed our old habit of spending time together in the evenings.

I practised drawing and painting more vigorously, exploring new styles, experimenting with watercolour and pen-and-ink, oils, scraper board and whatever The New Stationary Mart recommended. I eagerly bought supplies and tried them out.

I discovered the use of a mirror to study the shape of my hand, fingers, legs, eyes, ears, the folds that formed in the pants when one sat cross-legged and so on.

Once I leaned a large mirror against the wall, sat in front of it and drew a portrait of myself in great detail, shading it to give it depth and texture. I thought I had done a marvellous job. Each time I saw it I touched it up a bit here and there. One day, irresistibly moved by some reckless whimsy, I added a moustache. I went further and added a beard. I looked like a sadhu. But the portrait needed long unkempt hair to complete the picture of a holy man. I drew kumkum on his forehead to provide the finishing touch. Later I tucked it away among my other sketches and forgot all about it.

Life went on smoothly till news began to trickle in that there were cases of typhoid in certain nearby villages. Soon there were rumours that it had arrived in Mysore. It was confirmed by a couple of boys in the college falling ill and being admitted to the hospital in a critical condition.

At the time Mahatma Gandhi gave the 'Quit India' call I was fighting a battle of my own for survival, having caught the virulent infection. When I hazily saw Mother leaning over my bed and peering at me anxiously one day, I did not realize that more than a month had gone by since I had last seen her. Only that morning I had shown some hopeful signs of recovery, having been almost unconscious till that time.

As time passed I got better. I picked up tit-bits of news of the outside world from people who came to see me, gathered around my bed and chatted. I learned that schools and colleges had been closed as the students look a big hand in the fight to rid the country of the British rule. My friend HK had been arrested and put in jail. I could never imagine that this could have happened to such a mild and soft-spoken fellow! He had joined what was called the 'Cycle Brigade', which meant cycling all over the town in groups, shouting anti-British slogans and courting arrest. I received a grubby looking postcard from HK. Two black bars on it censored something he had mentioned, which the jail superintendent had evidently thought was insulting to His Majesty the King Emperor! The uncensored part of the message described the poor standard of the prison library and the prison soup which seemed to be boiled from grass and stank of kerosene.

From other sources I heard about rioting, police brutalities and student deaths. These stories naturally aggravated the gloom in my sickroom. But occasionally there was comic relief. A friend of mine who was otherwise an intelligent and sensible chap strangely believed that the British should stay and continue to rule us, and that all talk of freedom was balderdash! He tactlessly aired these unpatriotic views, believing that he was being intellectually honest at a time when the national crisis needed a practical and common-sense approach. Once he overreached himself and referred to Mahatma Gandhi as 'Mr Gandhi with the spontaneity of Colonel Blimp!' The listeners around him who had been quietly amused and laughing, now turned on him with all the fury they could muster and he had to flee. He took refuge in the quarters occupied by Professor Eagleton. There he remained without venturing out till the general anger had abated, adding to his knowledge of Milton, Macaulay and Burke, learning from the professor at first hand.

And there was another friend of mine who was a born idealist. He harassed the police in various non-violent Gandhian ways, and tormented the jail authorities by ceaselessly asking them to adhere strictly to jail manual rules. Released from the city jail after a prolonged imprisonment, within a few hours he organized a group to help him to drag a gigantic weather-beaten temple chariot to a congested area. He parked it right in the middle of the road, blocking all traffic movement for several hours. Of course he was hauled back to prison; he went cheerfully, shouting anti-British slogans along with his supporters.

After hearing these stories I laughed so much that my sides literally ached and I developed breathing difficulty. I was advised to stay calm, and rest completely. I was not allowed any visitors.

Gradually I began to move around a little in the room itself, alternating between sitting at my table for some time and returning to bed. During my waking hours this was my only activity.

I used to open my desk drawers and my cupboards to

examine their contents. I took out and discarded cracked paint tubes, bottles of dried ink, any number of pencil stubs and damaged brushes. Then I collected my sketchbooks and sheets of drawings and arranged and filed them neatly. While I was doing this I found a portrait of a bearded man with long untrimmed hair and a large dash of kumkum on his forehead. I was astonished that the self-portrait I had playfully disfigured months ago turned out to resemble me as I looked at that very moment—beard and all—down to the kumkum Mother used to put on my forehead after offering prayers to the gods for my survival and recovery. It was a prophetic self-portrait, an astonishing case of intimation of my appearance foretold consequent on my near fatal illness. Everyone at home was astonished at my likeness to the portrait and came up with various conflicting theories about time, the fourth dimension and psychic phenomena.

It took a whole year for me to resume normal activity and return to college. One redeeming factor that emerged from this turbulent period was that my friend HK having lost a year fighting for freedom, I was able to catch up with him. We became bench-mates again!

*

I had a letter from a film studio in Madras soon after my BA exams were over, just as I was thinking of how best to spend my vacation. It was from a cartoonist who was toying with the idea of producing a cartoon film. He had been given the use of a studio, its staff and also some cash to meet his expenses. The cartoonist had taken on the roles of director and producer as well. He said he had seen my work in the

Hindu illustrating my brother's stories, and in a few other periodicals and thought I would ideally suit his requirement.

He offered me a salary of Rs 250 per month. I replied that I was ready to work for him, but alas, I could spare only three months as I was yet to complete my final year in college. To safeguard against his changing his mind and looking for a more permanent hand to help him, I added in the letter that I was visiting Madras anyway and that I would call on him when I was there.

I had no actual plans to go to Madras at that time of the year, when it would be hot like an inferno, especially after Mysore's mild weather. But I was curious to see his project. So I packed a bag and left. People at home wished me well and asked me to keep in touch. Mother said, 'Don't wander around in the sun. The April sun in Madras is veritable fire. Don't fail to take an oil bath every week. That will cool the system . . .'

In Madras I stayed with an aunt in a bungalow so huge that it absorbed my presence quietly and no one felt that a guest was around.

The very day of my arrival I went to the film studio to see the director of the cartoon unit. He seemed very pleased to see me. He explained how the idea of the film had first come into his mind, what plans he had, how far he had progressed. He was so excited and spoke so rapidly that sometimes I missed what he was saying. It was all a chaotic jumble of technical details, financial implications and creative ideas. He called his staff one by one and introduced me. Then he ordered a peon to fetch a table and a chair and to put them in a corner of his own room. After seating me at the table he made me sign some papers appointing me as a temporary staff member in charge of key drawings. He said he would explain what that was later.

Then he said the story was written by a full-time actor, a comedian featuring in movies produced by this studio. My heart sank when I heard the name, for I had seen him in several movies. Further shock came when I learnt that the cartoon film was based on the mythological character Naradamuni: a bearded saint, clutching a single-stringed instrument all the time, strumming it and singing while he was not intriguing with the gods in heaven. He was a great character in our mythology no doubt, but it was revolting to think of him as a cartoon character. Judging from the writer's concept of humour, I knew how grotesque and crude the storyline would be.

I was shown a few specimen drawings of the main character. There was no attempt at stylizing of human form as one found in Disney's creations; humans were sketched in normal anatomical proportions. I wanted to express my opinion and make some critical remarks about their idea of humour. But I remained silent, acutely conscious that I was a total stranger in that place, and that I could not take the liberty of passing judgement on the strength of a two-hour acquaintance.

Besides, where to begin criticizing? The comedian writer and his idea? The characters they had chosen? The style of the drawings? Then I told myself that I had been invited simply to help them and not to bring about a revolution in the film unit to suit my taste. I had been appointed as the key drawing artist and I had better stick to that. These thoughts helped me to control my impatience and listen attentively to the director as he narrated the story.

Narada was floating about in heaven singing, moving self-propelled from the abode of one god to another, scheming and gossiping. He slipped on a step and rolled down helplessly till he fell into space. He landed on a patch of cloud which gave way, so Narada plummeted straight towards the earth. On reaching where he crashed through the roof of a haircutting saloon and collapsed into a barber's swivel chair. Under the impact, the chair revolved so fast that Narada became giddy. The barber, unaware of the identity of the heavenly customer, automatically tied a sheet around Narada's neck and proceeded to give him a haircut and clean shave. Mercifully, the story ended there; the rest was still being written.

I was appalled by the reaction of the studio hands who were standing around and listening to the director's narration. They guffawed loudly, excitedly thumped each other's backs and laughed at Narada's fall from heaven and his plight in the barber's chair.

I wondered how I was to spend three months in the company of people whose sense of humour so outraged me. Having signed the contract and accepted the commission to be the key animator, I had no way of retracing my steps to Mysore and enjoying the company of my friend HK.

I reconciled myself to the intellectual and aesthetic standards of my studio colleagues, and started work the very next day.

The director had accorded me special status and I shared his room with him. He was also good enough to make what was a complicated business easy for me. I was just to draw a character tumbling down a hundred steps of a staircase that led to heaven.

I visualized a man in dhoti and upper cloth flailing his arms, kicking his legs and hitting his behind against the steps. I made a few pencil sketches and I showed them to the director. He was so excited he rang the bell and summoned all the staff to view my efforts. They stood around and clucked their tongues in appreciation. The director asked me to create further oddities and variations in Narada's fall.

I did not know the technicalities of this medium. I learnt that there were twenty-four drawings per second and the sequence of the fall from the steps would last about forty seconds. That meant it would take around a thousand sketches for the single episode of Narada rolling down! The editor watched my expression of astonishment with amusement and assured me that I did not have to sweat over all the thousand sketches. Just a few key drawings would do. Guided by these his artists would create the illusion of motion.

I spent over eight hours in the studio every day. I watched the artist redraw my sketches in a serial form to show action. Then these would be transferred on to transparent celluloid sheets for cranking frame by frame through a movie camera.

When I went back home at night, I also took the trouble of enacting an actual fall down a staircase when no one was looking. I carefully took notes of my observations; the angle of the hand trapped under the body, the twist of the limbs, facial grimaces and so on. Later I incorporated these authentic details as I worked on drawing after drawing.

The most exciting moment was when the shooting was finally over, and the film developed and ready. The director asked everyone to gather in the editing room to view the film on the mini-screen of a moviola.

After months of sweating over the production, creative agonies, discussions, heated arguments, the thrill of watching the fruits of our labour lasted less than fifteen seconds showing some jerky movements on the screen.

Disappointment was writ large on the faces of the viewers. The editor tried to boost our morale by assuring that with the background music it would come out splendidly. Someone said that on the big screen it would even look grand! Thus there was a babble of suggestions and counter-suggestions about editing and re-takes.

As for me the whole business seemed an anticlimax beyond redemption. But I kept my opinion to myself, nodding my agreement generally with a genial smile at whoever looked in my direction. I was only interested in my salary, the excellent opportunity I had to practice sketching, and the superb free lunch provided by the studio canteen.

After working for over a month I had yet to come to the point where Narada would be launched into outer space on his disastrous journey to earth.

At this time there was a welcome diversion from the tedious business of preparing key drawings. The all-India postal strike by employees demanding higher wages was on. Negotiations for a settlement had fallen through. As I read the news item a brilliant idea for a cartoon struck me. It was irresistibe. I took time off from Narada and produced the cartoon. But I did not know whom to offer it to. I was too timid to take it to the *Hindu* or the *Express*. Just then I remembered a friend who knew the editor of a monthly called *Swarajya*. With his help I finally stood before the editor in his office. He saw my cartoon and accepted it straightaway, saying it came just in time to catch the latest issue of *Swarajya*, which would be out in a couple of days. He offered me fifty rupees very apologetically, saying this was the best payment he could afford!

Events had moved so rapidly since the moment the idea for the cartoon occurred to me, that I did not have the time to gather myself and wake up from the dreamy state I was in. What finally woke me up was another pleasant shock the editor administered! He said if I agreed he would like to have a cartoon from me every month for *Swarajya*.

I had contributed two cartoons and collected a hundred rupees by the time Narada bounced off a passing cloud. I returned to Mysore leaving him gyrating in the barber's chair where I had made him land.

Many years later I visited the Disney studio in Hollywood. It was spread over several acres and looked like a vast factory. Thousands of artists, directors and workers were employed in creating Mickey Mouse and his companions. There were over two hundred artists, mostly women, employed only to copy the sketches onto celluloid. I remembered the Madras studio where just five were engaged for this particular job.

I was very eager to meet Walt Disney, whose contribution to the make-believe world of animated beings no one had surpassed. But when I met him it was a disappointment. He talked like an industrial tycoon and corporate giant, rather than an artist with a truly stunning imagination.

*

My last year in college went off rather uneventfully. At least that's how it seems now, when I look back on it, having to rely on my rather feeble memory. I'm not in the habit of keeping notes about any event, big or small.

All I can vaguely recall are features of some of the professors, having sketched them many times over when the lectures got tedious. The boy sitting next to me would be thrilled by a guessing game I had started. I would draw just a circle and two tiny dots in the middle. He would view it with suppressed laughter and utter, 'Iyengar'. That would be the economic history lecturer. Then I would draw a long nose without a face; that would be 'Acharya', the philosophy teacher. An egg-shaped oval—Professor Eagleton for Shakespeare, and so on. I could draw all these only in the safety of the crowded senior BA hall, a vast room accomodating nearly two hundred students! Our desks were arranged in ascending levels, so no teacher had any idea of who was who in the back rows at the top! HK and I generally favoured the rear desks.

All my thoughts now were on my future career and getting out of college, with or without a Bachelor of Arts degree! I already had a little income from my regular freelance work. Besides, I had also been commissioned to do minor projects, such as advertisements for toilet soap or posters to promote adult literacy.

My mind used to wander a great deal in the classroom and I often doodled idly or took out a blade and carved my initials on the desk. There were quite a few similar inscriptions on every desk left by other bored and restless minds. I used to speculate about NKB, CRS, L RAO, GK . . . and wondered where they might be at that moment. Some of of the initials, for example CRS, were found on many desks in almost every room in the college. This fellow's sole purpose seemed to have been to come to college just to carve his name and get out! These desks were nearly a hundred years old, and those who had left their imprints must have been dead and gone.

The weather was getting warmer, heralding the summer and the approach of examinations. I was sitting in the senior BA hall in the last row, listening to a lecture on money and banking. The resonance of the teacher's voice made me sleepy. My eyes wandered dreamily across the surface of the desk. Suddenly I thought I saw very familiar initials, RKP. That was my brother Pattabhi! Below that was RKN, followed by RKS, RKB, and RKR. All my brothers at various stages of their passage through the portals of Maharaja's college had discovered this part of the desk and left their names. And, of course, I etched RKL below the last one and completed the genealogy.

I faced the final year (of my examination) with a certain casual resignation, for I had decided I would make only one attempt to pass and bid goodbye to education. Just two weeks after the exams ended I packed up and left Mysore. I had already bought a large brown steel trunk into which I dumped all my possessions, books, drawing material, papers and clothes. I painted my name in block letters on the lid of the box and I was all set to depart.

My elders as usual generously cheered me on my way into the world.

My destination was Madras, and my plan was to get a job in one of the newspapers. I was too timid to approach the *Hindu* as they were already using David Low's syndicated cartoons. So I decided to try the *Indian Express.* But I knew no one there. Nevertheless I walked into the office one morning and went to the nearest desk in the editorial department. An elderly man was ploughing through sheaves of galley proofs. I told him why I was there and showed him some clippings of my published cartoons. He went through them with bemused interest. Meanwhile I was getting more and more certain that my letter of appointment would be handed over to me at any moment. When the man had finished he handed over the cartoons, shaking his head and saying that there was no opening for a political cartoonist in the *Express.* He went on mumbling something about disgruntled staff, a mean proprietor and the possibility of a strike. I was greatly disappointed, and left.

Then I thought of calling on my old friends at the film studio where I had done my stints at animating Narada. The director was delighted to see me. He offered me a chair, fussed about adjusting the fan and ordered idli and coffee from the famous studio canteen.

He asked about my future plans. On the spur of the moment I said that I was on my way to Delhi, an idea which was vaguely germinating in my mind. I was actually afraid he would again invite me to tackle the key drawings for the cartoon film. I could see some artists working in the next room. He told me some of the artists had left and production had been delayed.

The director narrated the rest of the story, following the barber's-chair incident. 'Narada runs away from the saloon, beardless. Not being familiar with this world, coming as he did from heaven, he is scared of the madly-honking cars, lorries and buses, and runs helter-skelter to escape from them. Then he sees a postbox. Thinking it is an earthling, he asks it for directions back to heaven.' At this point the director could not control himself and began to laugh uproariously. I joined him sniggering out of politeness and asked how the boss, meaning the owner of the studio, liked the film. I was told he appreciated it very much. The director offered to introduce me to him.

The boss seemed a very cultivated type, unlike others in his profession. He had neither whiskers nor sideburns; nor was his manner aggressive. I was introduced to him as a cartoonist and a brother of R.K. Narayan, who had supervised the studio production of a couple of his novels. The boss was eager to see my work. I showed him the cartoons I had taken that morning to the *Express* office. He was very impressed with them and immediately offered to employ me on the staff of the humorous weekly he brought out which was a household name in the Tamil-speaking world. I was torn between the impulse to accept a job offered to me on a platter, so to speak, and the temptation to test my luck with some English publications in Delhi. The boss sensed my dilemma and generously told me there was no hurry about it. Whenever I decided I wanted the job, I could join. His doors were always open to me.

Thus, with a readymade job to fall back upon if I failed in my attempts in Delhi, I boarded the Grand Trunk Express and left Madras.

The younger of my two elder sisters lived in Delhi. She was married to S.A. Venkataraman, an ICS officer. He was secretary in the department of industry and commerce, and lived as befitting his status in a big bungalow surrounded by a lawn with a tennis court, garden and ancient trees. I stayed in this house during my sojourn in Delhi.

I found it difficult to adjust to Delhi. A mournful atmosphere pervaded the whole city. The trees lining the broad avenues stood at cheerless attention, like regimented soldiers. I was accustomed to Mysore's trees, which had personality and individuality, whimsical branches, varieties of colour. But most of the trees in Delhi lacked charm. Even the residential houses seemed impersonal and cold, perhaps due to the fact that they were government quarters and therefore lacked the warmth of homeliness. These were my reactions in the early days after my arrival at Delhi when I used to wander about alone pondering and reflecting over my observations.

But the house I lived in was vast, comfortable and lively. My sister had a large circle of friends and constant visitors. Most of the evenings there were cocktail and dinner parties. I used to get a glimpse of the guests through a chink in my bedroom door. But I joined the guests and sipped cocktails when the party included common friends of the family. Some of them I got to know better after meeting them in their offices or at India Coffee House. Unfortunately none of them had gone anywhere near a newspaper office nor had any idea of its working and the need for a cartoonist in that setup. Still I poured out my heart to them. Some of them promised to help me.

One morning I got a call at home from one of these Coffee House friends, asking me to come to the department of health and education in the government secretariat. He said he had some good news for me. Immediately I borrowed our peon's bicycle, jumped on to it and pedalled away towards South Block as fast as I could. I was bewildered by the maze of corridors, the staircases, the stately pillars, the peons in vintage raj-style uniforms with gold braid and red cummerbunds. Finally I located my friend. He was just one among dozens who sat at tables cluttered with files. He escorted me to a room down the corridor; I guessed that it was the office of the assistant secretary in the department of health and education. He sat in a spacious room all by himself behind a large desk, in a luxurious leather-upholstered chair. My friend left us after the introductions.

The official surprised me by speaking in Kannada. He told me he was from Mysore and knew my family, father, brothers and so on and had seen my work in some Kannada publications. He wanted a poster designed by me. The theme was tuberculosis. The poster should aim at instilling civic sense in people to prevent the disease from spreading. The accompanying slogan was: *Coughing in crowded places is deadly. Cover your mouth with a handkerchief and save lives!*

Deep inside me at that moment a voice cried out, 'Oh God, have I come all the way from Mysore and Madras to Delhi to participate in eradicating TB?' I wondered if I would ever get a chance to draw political cartoons, distort the faces of leaders, bringing out the ironies and paradoxes in political events, reveal politicians for the buffoons they were! Or was

I doomed to work all my life educating people about malaria, cholera, jaundice?

However, I left the secretary's room with a great show of enthusiasm for the assignment with a bundle of literature on tuberculosis which he so kindly presented to me.

In a couple of days I had prepared the poster, complete with the slogan '*Coughing in public* . . .' The assistant secretary was immensely satisfied. I had shown a large face of a man, contorted coughing, his mouth releasing a spray composed of lethal tiny bombs over a cityscape.

After leaving my work with the official, I did not see him again. Never was I told about the fate of the poster.

*

Suddenly my luck took a turn for the better. At a cocktail party at home my brother-in-law introduced me to the editor of the *Hindustan Times*. After a few ritual questions and answers he invited me to see him in his office the following morning. I was so excited by the prospect that I could not sleep that night. I kept tossing from side to side, sitting up, walking round the cot, peering at the clock-face in the dark dozens of times before daybreak.

I was at the editor's ante-room for visitors half an hour before the appointment. He arrived smiling and stretched out his hand for a warm handshake. I was flattered because a few others also waiting for him looked at me with curiosity.

I liked him—his friendly nature appealed to me. He studied my collection of cartoons with concentration. I could see he was assessing my political understanding and sense of irony. After scrutinizing them carefully he put them aside and told me that although my work was of a high standard, he could not offer me a job. They already had a veteran staff cartoonist who had been with them for years, and might be offended if I were to share the column of the paper him with. It was a valid reason and I appreciated the straightforward way the editor dealt with the matter. He suggested I should meet the cartoonist and have a casual chat with him. Perhaps there was a chance of the cartoonist himself wanting me to join the paper.

I was already familiar with this man's work. He churned out undistinguished cartoons without any political depth, verve of draftmanship, or satirical essence. I never heard anyone taking note of his cartoons or discussing them. I felt that people just read the news surrounding the cartoon, without looking at it. But to make up for this, the cartoonist was, I soon found, an extremely warm-hearted fellow.

He laughed when he went through my portfolio and appreciated each cartoon without reservation. But he said that I should first work in a provincial newspaper for some time before aspiring to try my chances in the capital. It was a clear indication that he wanted me out of the way. Perhaps he even had a suspicion that I was calling on the editor to get into the paper.

The next person I met was the proprietor of the *Indian Express*. He introduced me to one of his senior editors in Delhi. The man lived in an apartment in Connaught Circus. I lost no time in locating the place, standing at his door, and ringing the bell. There was no response for a long time. Just as I was about to leave I sensed some movement on the other side of the door. When it clicked open an elderly man with dishevelled grey hair appeared frowning at the bothersome afternoon glare. The interior of the flat was totally dark. I mentioned my business. He invited me in, went straight into what was his bedroom and lay down, pulling a thick rug up to his nose. He asked me to pull up a chair and sit next to his cot in the semi-darkness. I explained the purpose of my visit, my ambition, my experience and other sundry details which I could reel off without effort, having repeated all this many times by now to various people in various places at various times. He listened with his eyes shut without any comment. Even when I finished my biodata and lapsed into silence he did not stir. The smell of beer which hung in the air, the darkness of the room and the inert body with which I was carrying on a one-sided conversation oppressed me. I felt like slipping out without taking leave. Suddenly the man startled me by saying, 'Why do you want to be a cartoonist? What is so great about it? Why not take up some other job? Why a cartoonist!' He delivered the advice without opening his eyes.

At this point I got up and quietly left. Perhaps he did not even notice my departure.

The disappointment in not being able to get into the *Express* and the insult I had to suffer from the somnambulant editor faded from my memory over the years. Eventually I became the political cartoonist for the *Times of India*.

I became quite active. People looked forward to and appreciated my cartoons. Some foreign newspapers—the *New York Times*, the *Times* of London, and some German publications began to reproduce some of my cartoons. Many years later I received a message informing me that the Express Group of papers was pleased to confer on me the B.D. Goenka award consisting of a lakh of rupees and a citation for my professional excellence! I could not help recalling the admonition of the editor in his smelly, dark bedroom, 'Why do you want to be a cartoonist? What's so great about it? . . .' nearly two decades earlier.

Equally ironically, I was also honoured with the Durga Ratan Gold Medal, an award given in memory of the editor of the *Hindustan Times* who had treated me so kindly when I met him but was regretfully unable to accommodate me in his paper.

I journeyed to Bombay just to hault for a week for sight-seeing before pushing off to Madras to accept the job in the Tamil weekly which had already been offered to me.

I knew no one in Bombay except a sub-editor working in the *Bombay Chronicle*. He was good enough to keep me company and show me round the city.

I found the place enchanting and cheerful, although the roads were dug up and there were slums and jostling crowds everywhere. The atmosphere was vibrant, people seemed busy round the clock, in contrast to my impressions of Delhi.

I loved the Arabian Sea, the sands of Chowpatty, the Malabar Hill, the tall buildings. I found the time move rather fast. Three days had already flashed past like objects seen through a moving train window. The thought that I had to leave for Madras in another three days brought a lump to my throat.

In one of our wanderings we were just passing by the *Blitz* office and my friend suggested calling on the editor. He was bold, liberal, generous and always rankled like a thorn at the side of authority. His publication was very popular and read widely if only for its tinge of sensationalism.

Almost as soon as we met, he suggested that I do a

cartoon strip on the notorious Kalbadevi shooting. It was a dastardly case of murder in broad daylight in the busy streets of Kalbadevi. Just before the Partition of India two offenders who had been imprisoned for murder and looting escaped from prison, stole arms from an arms depot, hired a taxi and drove down the Kalbadevi road, opening fire right and left with a machine gun. When the driver panicked and stopped the taxi he was shot too. They jumped out of the vehicle and disappeared. During this short journey they left dead in their wake a jeweller inside his shop, a schoolchild, a vegetable seller, a customer in a tea shop and also several injured pedestrians.

A few days later the police traced the culprits. The court tried them and they were sentenced to death. At about the time I arrived in Bombay they were hanged. It was a sensational news all over the city.

The editor told me this story briefly and gave me papers concerning the trial. He wanted a pictorial narration of the incident to run as a serial each week. He offered to pay me a thousand rupees a month. It was a lot of money, and with the regular cheque from *Swarajya* I could remain in Bombay for a fairly long time. He offered an escort to take me through the area of the gory shootings, and also to introduce me to some of the eyewitnesses and those who suffered bullet injuries.

I was first taken to Kalbadevi street. It was a busy congested thoroughfare about half a kilometre long. Buses, cars, bicycles, pushcarts and pedestrians were all moving up and down in grand disorder. Booksellers, watch repairers, barber saloons, teashops and silversmiths were lined up on either side of the street. I thought of the massacre that had taken place many years earlier, and shuddered at my vision of the panic that the spluttering guns from the taxi must have created that morning.

But it is a curious trick of memory that though I have been driving my car through Kalbadevi to reach my office every morning, I do not feel that I am the same person who shuddered with deep horror when he first saw the shops with bullet holes in their fixtures, and shopkeepers with bullet injuries. I had even driven through this street in the taxi that was used by the assassins, with the driver they had shot. After hitting him, a bullet had pierced the door of the taxi. He proudly showed me the hole.

I became busy preparing the cartoon strips and delivering them to the *Blitz* office. One day as I was returning a friend of mine took me down a side lane and showed me the office of the *Free Press Journal*. Just at that moment I saw someone getting out of a car and going into the building. My companion told me this was the editor of the *Free Press* and would I like to be introduced to him? There was not a second of hesitation on my part. A moment later I was sitting before the editor, rattling off my biography right up to the point of meeting him. He was already familiar with my work, thanks to *Swarajya*.

I joined the *Free Press Journal* as its political cartoonist for the grand salary of two hundred and fifty rupees per month. It was not the money, I told myself, it was the opportunity to work in a newspaper office. I did a variety of work for the paper, far beyond what the salary justified. I did a political cartoon every alternate day, a three-in-one illustrated comment for the Sunday paper, a cartoon strip containing light social jokes, story illustrations for the magazine section and numerous others for the pages called the State's People Supplement. I used to sit bent over my drawing board for nearly ten hours a day.

Besides me there were two other cartoonists sitting next to me, pouring out their creative genius, attacking, lampooning and ridiculing the political leaders.

One of the cartoonists was Bal Thackeray. He was competent and efficient but was preoccupied with the idea of saving Maharashtra, its prestine glory, people, language and culture. Gradually he relegated the business of cartooning to the background and became an active politician, heading a party of his own as its supremo. He turned out to be a formidable factor to reckon with in state politics.

The proprietor of the *Free Press Journal* was a strong nationalist, a devout Gandhian and deeply religious. Once when he had gone to the USA he flew back for just a day to perform some puja, and returned to America the next morning.

One day his confidential secretary secretly showed me an album of photographs of sheer fantasy. The first photograph showed the proprietor standing on the orb of the earth looking heavenward, with palms pressed together in an attitude of prayer to the plethora of gods congregated in the sky. Their hands were raised in the traditional posture of blessing. Rays of light emanated from each divine palm, reached out to the proprietor below on earth and set him aglow. Of course, the whole panorama was a cleverly superimposed and touched-up business on a photograph.

The rest of the photographs in the album were all similarly fabricated, showing the proprietor close to the gods, getting individual attention and blessing.

But the office staff dreaded him. He had a permanent angry expression and a temperament to go with it. On the flimsiest grounds he would sack entire squads of clerks, sub-editors, editors, reporters and peons at one go, without batting an eyelid. He had a personal astrologer who visited off and on. The sacking orders usually followed his visit. Once the proprietor sent an eager young journalist to Beirut to start an exclusive international news bureau. The young man packed up all his things and left. But on reaching his destination he received a letter informing him that he had been sacked. He had to repack all his possessions and somehow find the money for the return journey since the head office did not respond to his cry for help. Many months later he walked into the office thin and unshaven.

There were quite a few people in the *Free Press Journal* office who resigned before being sacked. Thus at one time or another almost all the journalists working in various other newspapers and periodicals in Bombay had been on the staff of the *Free Press Journal*.

One day my childhood friend HK suddenly appeared at the office. We had graduated from college together. He had collected his degree and gone to Madras to do postgraduate study in economics. Although I was informed that I had passed, I never collected my degree. Even now it must be gathering dust somewhere in the archives of the university registrar's office.

HK looked cheerful and prosperous. A cigarette dangled from his lips. He was holding an expensive cigarette tin and lighter. I was overjoyed to see him. I dropped all work and went out with him to a restaurant. Later we went and saw a movie and had dinner together. We gossiped about old friends and described our various experiences over the years.

He said he was making a lot of money at the stock exchange buying, selling and bidding through an agent. My friend was wearing a smart suit and carrying a briefcase. Somehow it seemed uncharacteristic of HK to dress like a stockbroker's assistant. As I knew him his attempt was to appear like an indifferently dressed dishevelled intellectual.

I had taken a room as a paying guest on the ground floor of a five-storey building on Marine Drive. HK used to drop in occasionally during weekends. He himself was staying in a hotel in Juhu.

When the clouds gathered and rains lashed the city in the month of June, I lost touch with him for several weeks. But one night when I had secured the windows and gone to bed, and was listening in the dark to the patter of rain, in a half-dreamy state I thought I heard faintly someone calling me: 'RK, RK.' I got up and saw HK standing outside, completely soaked. I called him in. He was drenched to the skin and was in a sad state. I helped him to dry himself, gave him a change of clothes and made him sleep in my bed. He was tired and went to sleep immediately. I sat up the whole night in a chair. In the early hours of the morning I heard him mumbling that he had lost all his money in the stock exchange. His agent had cheated him. After this announcement he fell into a deep sleep. I went to my office and made a call to his elder brother in Delhi, describing HK's condition. By the time I came back from work my friend had left for Juhu.

I found him in a poky hotel. His room was dark and the bed unmade, his clothes were scattered all over the place. He did not seem to have had a decent meal in a long time. He sounded incoherent. While talking, he cried and laughed alternately.

When his brother arrived from Delhi he called on me at the *Free Press Journal*. I told him what had happened to HK and took him to Juhu. Then I arranged for rail bookings to Bangalore and saw them off at the station.

Later I heard that HK underwent psychiatric treatment and was finally admitted to the asylum in Bangalore. While being given an injection to calm him down he passed away.

At the office my turn to leave the *Free Press* was not long in coming. But I pre-empted the boss and took him by surprise.

I had heard rumours that he had struck a deal with a political party to support its ideology, its style of functioning without reservation unquestioningly. It was whispered that in return the party would rescue him from the financial crisis he was facing. By then the editor who had appointed me had left and the proprietor himself took over the business of editing the paper. Soon an editorial by him appeared, surprising the readers. It shamelessly showered praise on the very party which until a few days ago the paper had attacked relentlessly. Photographs of the party leaders were made a must whenever a news item about them appeared.

But I continued to develop my critical comments, made fun of these leaders and ridiculed their mindless followers. The editor naturally found this contradiction in editorial views embarrassing. He summoned me to his office and ordered me to mend my ways and toe the policy of the paper. He sensed my reluctance to obey him. I was expecting he would ask me to get out of the office. But curiously, he suggested in a very kind tone that as an alternative I could continue to illustrate stories and produce harmless sketches if I gave up drawing satirical cartoons on current politics.

I grunted something in reply and left the room with my head bent, not looking up at him. I went straight to his personal assistant and asked him to type a two-line resignation note and sent it in. On seeing it he must have felt cheated of a chance to sack a staff member, and sent for me again. He told me not to be foolish and asked me to take back my resignation. Finding me rather adamant, he scribbled instructions to the accounts department to settle my dues strictly up to date. There were just three days till the end of the month. I collected my salary of about Rs 134 and stepped out into Dalal Street.

There was a taxi strike that day, so I climbed into a victoria and rode in grand style to the *Times of India* office, which luckily I did not have to leave for more than half a century.

I knew no one in the *Times* office. But I walked in and asked at the reception for the editorial department.The whole place seemed such a contrast to the *Free Press Journal* office. Most of the staff were English. I found everyone polite, smiling and spruce. There was silence except for the clatter of typewriters. Everyone wore ties and jackets. They were walking up and down, making polite noises wishing each other 'Thanks', 'Hello' and 'Morning' through teeth clutching the pipe.

Finally I was shown into a waiting room. It had a few gold-framed oil paintings on the wall. I remember one of them was by a Greek named Bagtapolous. It depicted the dying Shah Jahan in his balcony, watching his creation, the

Taj Mahal. This painting still adorns one of the executive rooms in the *Times* office.

An attendant asked, 'Mr Laxman? Cartoonist? You have to go to the art department.' I had written on my visitor's slip: *Profession: Cartoonist.* So I was taken to the art director. This man had landed in Bombay a decade earlier from Vienna, fleeing from Hitler. Thanks to the British he had found a job in the *Times* as the director in the art department. He had an intimidating appearance—he was tall, heavily built, blond, blue-eyed. His deep sonorous German accent matched his florid complexion, and his personality matched his rumbling, rhythmic name: Professor Walter Langhammar.

He was familiar with the profusion of cartoons I had drawn for the *Free Press Journal*. The first question he asked was if I copied David Low. I was taken aback. Resenting his allegation, I challenged him to test me. He gave me a sheet of paper, a pencil, brush and ink and asked me to draw a man sitting at a table. He left the room. I could see the sprawling art department through a large glass pane. There were about twenty artists engaged in illustrating stories for the *Illustrated Weekly*, comic strips for the children's magazine 'Junior', visuals and layouts for advertisements, touching up photographs and so on. I saw Langhammar with arms akimbo, pacing the aisles and carefully inspecting the work of artists.

He returned after a quarter of an hour. I had already completed the drawing. His pleasure was transparent. He was eager to employ me immediately. But he said he could not make me the political cartoonist for the *Times* because that was a matter concerning the editor. But he was ready to take me in his department to draw illustrations for the *Illustrated Weekly*, comic strips and other odd jobs. But no political cartoons! Once more in my life I was faced with the dilemma between what I wanted to do and what I was asked to do. I could not afford to reject the opportunity. I told myself I would bide my time and realize my ambition some other day.

The professor was very happy that I accepted his offer. He asked me what salary I expected and what I had been getting in my previous job. 'Rs 250,' I replied. 'And what do you expect now?' I announced that I expected Rs 350. He looked amused and left the room. When he came back he brought a letter with him and gave it to me. It was an appointment letter. He had raised my salary to Rs 500!

So I plunged into work. An Agatha Christie story was being serialized for the *Weekly* and I was assigned to illustrate it. I also created a comic strip called 'Gutta-Percha' for the Junior magazine. It was about a little boy and a baby elephant and their adventures week after week.

On the whole I worked in a pleasant atmosphere with friendly fellow artists. But my heart was still set on political cartoons. Somehow I could never get rid of the feeling that what I was doing just then was temporary.

To break the monotony of work, the professor had arranged with the neighbouring JJ School of Arts to supply models for life classes once a week for us to improve our skills. These models were standard types—a bearded sadhu, an old man with a turban, a young working girl holding a pot on her hip. These models posed sitting on a stool or standing, according to our requirements for sketching.

One day when the model arrived the professor stepped out of his cubicle and bellowed in his deep gruff voice,

'Nude!' I was shocked to see the lady who had arrived disrobe immediately and calmly assume an artistic pose without a stitch on her body.

Some days later a well-polished table was brought into the department and put in a corner. The Professor strode towards me and shook my hand, announcing that it had been specially ordered for me! It was of a normal size, with drawers and a slanting drawing board. I still have the same table today, despite all attempts by the office to persuade me to use a bigger and better one.

*

I knocked about for a couple of months, getting familiar with the vibrant metropolis and making new friends. But I was becoming tired of living as a paying guest. The apartment I stayed in belonged to a government official and he was alone in the spacious flat, having left his family in his hometown. I hardly saw him, for he was constantly away on tours.

One day I decided to shift to a hotel. I found an ideal one called 'Hotel Mirabel'. It was in a street bustling with activity round the clock. The proprietor was a man from Udipi, the home of culinary art.

The lobby of the hotel was always full of interesting characters walking in and out. Mirabel had rented out its rooms to lodgers as well as offices. The second floor had the office of the 'Buyer Meets Seller', a second-hand car dealer; next to it was a travel agency, then an astrologer who also doled out medicines in the form of herbs, powders and dried and pounded leaves.

The other rooms in the hotel were occupied by

employees of business houses, and travelling sales representatives who had rented rooms hoping to find their own accommodation some day. But since Bombay's housing shortage was very acute, they had practically become permanent tenants.

My room was large and comfortable. My circle of friends began to increase. The lodgers in other rooms, the manager, the accountants and clerks used to drop in for a chat. The proprietor and I became particularly close. My time in Mirabel was a fascinating period of experience. I gathered enough material here for a novel which I wrote later, called *The Hotel Riviera*.

On the whole I led a trouble-free and interesting life both at the *Times of India* and outside. But as days passed the thought that I was not doing the job I was cut out for began to gnaw at my conscience. There was no mental challenge in illustrating stories for the *Weekly*, or comic strips for children's magazines. I felt that my intellectual capacity was getting atrophied, and that I was losing the sharp satirical perspective and eye for absurdity which form the soul of a political cartoon.

Such constant introspection made me despair, particularly when I happened to read the newspaper report of a minister's speech which was just made for cartooning. And sometimes those who used to admire my work in my *Free Press Journal* days asked me when my cartoons would start appearing in the *Times of India*. Those were my worst moments. When I could not contain the self-inflicted torment any longer I started to draw political cartoons just for my own satisfaction. One day I boldly walked into the editor's ante-room and told the PA I had to see his boss urgently. The editor was British, an ex-army man who had seen action on the Burma front. I braced myself to face the brusque, abrupt style of a British Army Officer like the characters I used to see in the war movies.

But this man was extremely nice. He made me sit down and paid undivided attention when I poured out my woes. But I was sure there was no chance that he would he moved and let me do the cartoons for the *Times*. So as I had planned, I offered to draw cartoons for his eyes only, and get some valuable comments. I told him this would enable me to keep in touch with my art and also to benefit from his critical assessment. He pondered over my rather unusual suggestion for a while and said that I was not big enough yet to take on the role of a political cartoonist for the *Times*. Expressing perhaps his personal admiration for my work, he observed, without any apparent connection to our dialogue, that Winston Churchill did not become great overnight, or something to that effect. But he gladly agreed to the arrangement that I draw political cartoons not for publication but just for him to view.

I immediately set about drawing. I submitted cartoons to him every alternate day. Some days he merely smiled at them, some days he grunted, 'Jolly good', or asked me to explain the satirical content. Occasionally he laughed and called the assistant editors next door by tapping on the frosted glass partition, to share the provocation in the cartoon.

This went on for some time and I was piling up unpublished cartoons in my drawer. Another period of gloom and depression was setting in. Then one morning the editor asked me to fetch the cartoon I had done the previous day. I think it was something about the Berlin blockade. The next day I was delighted to see it appear in our evening paper, the *Evening News of India*. Following this, I started contributing to the *Evening News*. A few weeks later the editor called for a cartoon I had done on the World Bank's niggardly loan to India. It appeared in the *Times of India* on the front page. From then on I began to draw cartoons three times a week for the *Times*, with a panel of three cartoons on Sunday. This routine I have stuck to for the past half century.

*

Meanwhile the proprietorship of Bennett, Coleman & Co. Ltd. changed to Indian hands. The British staff was gradually eased out and Indians were employed. I was shifted from the art to the editorial department, with the designation 'Chief Political Cartoonist of the *Times of India*'.

I continued to illustrate stories and articles for the *Weekly*, but now as a freelance contributor. I also started a feature called 'Personalities', in which I did full-page colour caricatures of prominent leaders in various walks of life, both in India and abroad.

Bombay became a permanent home. I decided to find a suitable accommodation and move out of the Mirabel Hotel. The shortage of housing was quite acute. The landlords were a greedy lot and had a merry time openly cheating helpless people looking for a roof over their heads and reducing them to bankruptcy. I had neither the time nor the experience to deal with these kinds of sharks and crooks. So I could make no headway. Besides doing cartoons for the *Times* I had taken on a lot of commissions, such as illustrating my brother's books, short stories, articles. I also did promotional drawings for commercial products for an advertising agency. I organized an exhibition of my cartoons and caricatures. I used to fly to Delhi frequently on official visits to meet political leaders, and sit in the parliament's press gallery to study the features and mannerisms of our political stalwarts.

This pattern of life moved with increasing momentum with each passing day. Absorbed in work, I had no free time to look for accommodation, which became an obsession and a nightmare. In the meanwhile, having married my niece, the pressure began to build up from my family now to set up a home without delay!

So I began to meet various agents and brokers. It led nowhere. They were not convinced about my solvency, nor was I of their integrity. At last, I found an agent who seemed honest and god-fearing. The time of our meeting seemed auspicious; he was sitting cross-legged on the floor meditating before a picture of a goddess. He acknowledged my presence by opening his eyes just a little and waved me to a chair. When he was ready he took me around the apartment to be rented. It was small and stuffy, with the bedroom, sitting room, bath, kitchen all in one room. I could not visualize my wife and I living in it. But I had no way out. We discussed the terms and I agreed to his demands. I left, telling him I would be back with the money, half by way of cheque and half in cash, the following day. I begged him not to give the flat away meanwhile to anyone else who was willing to pay more rent.

I calculated and found that the advance he was asking for would drain all I had saved over the years. But all the same I was relieved that I would have a place I could call my own.

That evening when I met the proprietor of the Mirabel for our usual gossip session, I mentioned that I would miss the atmosphere of the hotel when I moved to my own flat. He asked when I was moving, details of the location, the name of the agent, and so on.

The moment I mentioned the location his eyebrows shot up and he himself mentioned the name of the agent and described his looks, size and height. Then he laughed uproariously and said that the fellow was a big fraud. He had taken advance payment and rented out the same flat to ten other victims, who had no way of occupying the flat nor recovering the hefty sum they had paid!

So I continued to live in the Mirabel, helplessly waiting for a miracle. A few weeks later a family friend living in Madras called on me. He was a dignified elderly gentleman. I had not met him before, but he had heard of my plight and came to help. He had a flat in a posh area of Bombay. He kept it locked and used it only when he made his brief and rare business trips to the city. He offered me the key and invited me to stay in it till I found a place of my own.

I moved into the flat quickly. It was big and comfortably furnished. I hired a cook and a servant and invited my wife to join me at once.

This generous man who had let us use his flat had a business partner in Bombay who managed a timber factory in a sordid locality. There was always trouble in that area. Not a day passed without rival gangs indulging in fighting and murder. One day the police in their endless investigations found bloodstains outside the factory gate. Promptly they summoned the owner of the factory for questioning. Of course, nothing was proved. But our friend, his partner in Madras, was so shaken on hearing of the incident that he dissolved his partnership in Bombay, wound up his interests and left the city for good, transferring the flat to us. I have thus stayed in this flat for the past five decades. My son Srinivas grew up in it, graduated, joined the *Times* as its aviation correspondent, married Usha. Now I have a grand-daughter, Mahalaxmi!

*

In the years that followed we got sucked gradually into the vortex of the cocktail and dinner-party circuit. Lounge suit, bush-shirt or black tie, the invitation cards ordered, according to the status of the dignitaries being entertained. We were at the venue, in time, appropriately attired, to meet eminent lawyers, or doctors, or diplomats, or movie stars. In short, nearly everyone belonged to the elitist society in a metropolis of the importance of Bombay. It became a matter of either dining out or having people over at home for dinner.

We also went on regular holidays taking our son with us to Kashmir, Nepal, Sikkim and many far flung fascinating places. But in course of time the tempo of our social activity slowed down. We became more selective in accepting the invitations.

I congratulated myself on having achieved a harmonious routine—work, a couple of drinks in the evening at home in the company of my family, and retiring early to read in bed.

All this was shattered when Morarji Desai became the

chief minister of Maharashtra and introduced prohibition to snuff out what he perceived as the evil habit of drinking. It was said he would not even drink plain water to quench his thirst, but would prepare his own 'recycled liquid' from within himself and consume that!

While prohibition was intended to drive out the evil of drinking it welcomed in a big way, by the back door, the greater evils of illicit distillation, crime, corruption and smuggling.

People who had been generally indifferent to liquor now began to savour the thrill of breaking the law and drinking. The whole state was swarming with drunks tottering about at all odd hours. They were caught, arrested, fined, imprisoned. Police raids on the houses of the rich as well as the hutments of the poor were the order of the day.

As a law-abiding citizen I found myself literally left high and dry. But homes of foreigners and diplomats were comparatively safe from police raids, and I used to avail myself of their hospitality whenever it was offered; I never declined their invitations.

There were also people with one-bottle-a-month permits who bought twenty bottles at exhorbitant rates from smugglers and stored them under their cots, bringing them out to celebrate birthdays, marriages and so on. Thus smugglers who were once mere slum dwellers prospered enormously. But the chief minister fondly believed that fortune was smiling on them because of his prohibition policy. One of my cartoons of that time showed him on his rounds visiting slums. He comes across a man beaming with happiness and contentment, who tells him, 'It is good you introduced prohibition, sir. Your are truly our saviour. Just as you said, it has brought prosperity to our homes. Now my children are able to go to private schools, I take my family to hill stations during summer holidays and I myself am thinking of standing for the election, sir, with your blessing . . .'

I was once caught in a police raid. It was a New Year's eve party at the home of an Australian who worked in an advertising agency. Each flat in that ten-storey building was having a bash, and liquor was flowing freely. Our party had quite a few guests including chief executives of business firms, movie stars, a couple of diplomats from whom our guest must have got his supply of bottles for the party, and many other glittering socialites.

We all settled down to enjoy the merriment befitting the ushering in of the new year. I had hardly taken a sip from my glass when the doorbell rang and our hostess, expecting it to be some more guests, opened the door. In walked about half a dozen policemen led by an officer.

From that moment on till the early hours it was a time of prolonged humiliation and insult to human dignity. Our glasses were snatched away from our hands. Those guests who had taken refuge in the bedroom and toilets were rounded up and herded into the drawing room. Then we were ordered to stand in a row, and asked our names, addresses, qualifications, ages, where employed, if we had a liquor permit; if we did, we were asked to produce it. We were told that we would be driven to the police station in the waiting police van for a breath test. And we would be chargesheeted if found to have consumed alcohol.

Meanwhile the influential guests started frantically telephoning any acquaintances occupying seats of power; the home minister, the IG of police, Congress leaders, customs collectors and assorted other important entities. Calls went back and forth and finally we were let off, with the inspector warning us that we should be prepared to receive summons in due course for violating the prohibition law.

Next morning I woke up bleary-eyed and with a heavy head although I had not touched a drop of whisky on New Year's eve. I became a nervous wreck and swore I would not touch liquor as long as I lived. I dreaded the prospect of being dragged away to prison.

Providentially I was saved once more! I got a call from the state health minister's secretary. He said that the minister saw the list of people who were caught drinking the previous evening and he noticed mine among the name of the offenders. He conveyed the minister's advice that I should at once equip myself with a permit, regarding which he had spoken to the government medical doctor; I should go and see him. The secretary also gave me the good news that all the guilty souls had been let off the hook and there would be no trouble from the police.

The doctor whom I went to see for the permit at the government hospital took my weight and height, examined the colour of my tongue and jotted down his observations on a prescribed printed form. Then he asked me if I enjoyed liquor. I said rather shyly that indeed I did. He wrote *Habituated to drinking alcohol* on the form. He asked if I slept soundly at night or did I wake up in the middle of night and feel restless. But before I could answer he wrote *Insomnia*. Did my work require a lot of concentration and imagination? For that he recorded *Creative work*.

Finally I was granted a permit which allowed me a half

bottle of liquor or six bottles of beer a month! The doctor rather apologetically said that according to my age I was allowed only that much. But he added helpfully that the permit was just a legal safeguard and the quantity prescribed was only a formality.

Morarji Desai also banned horse racing and crossword puzzles. A cartoon I drew on this theme annoyed him so much that he held a full cabinet meeting to muzzle me, and ban making the government, politicians and ministers objects of ridicule in the name of humour. He was told there was no way of stopping the cartoons since our Constitution fully protected the freedom of expression.

The *Times of India* by now had a separate edition in Delhi. I was there when it started, and did a special series called, 'This is Delhi', making fun of local personalities. My usual political cartoons also appeared along with these sketches.

The management thought it would be a good idea to hold an exhibition of my cartoons, in an effort to boost the paper's circulation in the capital. So I gathered a selection from the eight years of my work illustrating national and international events. It was the first time such an exhibition was being held. It was inaugurated by an eminent person who was once our ambassador to the United States.

A large crowd had gathered for the opening, in response to the wide publicity created through posters, banners and announcements in the press. There were also special invitees to the function. Among them that evening was an eminent cartoonist who had become popular for his vitriolic humour that attacked the Imperial rulers, and for his patriotic support to the stalwarts of our freedom movement. I had met him earlier during my *Free Press Journal* days when he had come to Bombay scouting for talent for a humorous magazine he was planning to publish. He offered to take me under 'his wing', on a stipend of no more than fifty rupees!

The inaugural ceremony was arranged on the lawns outside the actual exhibition hall, which was too small to hold all the guests. When the chief guest arrived he was escorted straight to the dais without being shown even a glimpse of my work. He made a long speech extolling the political cartoon as one of the important checks and balances of power in a democracy. Then he caught sight of the veteran cartoonist in the front row. Pointing to him, he recounted how over the years this artist had ridiculed viceroys and bureaucrats with his mighty brush, and how his art drove home a lesson through his art to some of our wayward political leaders. The cartoonist became the centre of attraction that evening and all eyes admiringly turned to him.

After the speech was over the guest of honour was escorted inside the gallery by the resident editor of the *Times of India*, while I followed them with a fixed smile.

A large crowd poured into the hall, which soon filled with a subdued murmur. The chief guest stopped in front of some cartoons, examined others, asked questions about a few, which were answered by the resident editor. I heard some guffaws and laughter from the other end of the hall. I was happy the visitors were enjoying the show.

The dignitary finished viewing the cartoons and prepared to leave. We walked him to his waiting car. Before getting in he turned to me and asked where I had received my training. I told him I was entirely self-taught. He seemed surprised and complimented me on my proficiency, adding that there would be no difficulty at all in my getting a Fulbright scholarship if I applied for it. I thanked him for his advice and wondered what I would do with the scholarship, how was it to help me in developing my sense of humour, satirical attitude and a healthy irreverence in general!

When the crowd was still inside the hall, the veteran cartoonist stepped out and mumbled a few words of appreciation. As a budding cartoonist, he hoped I would not mind a piece of advice—if I wished to be successful, I should drop the Common Man with his striped coat, moustache and spectacles. He did not stop to explain how this poor man came in the way of my artistic development.

Not being in the habit of taking advice from anyone, I just carried on. But it was a pity that he was not alive to see, about three decades later, that the same Common Man was thought fit to adorn a postage stamp issued by the Indian government to commemorate the 150th anniversary of *Times of India*.

In the ten days the exhibition lasted I could sense a subtle critical assessment among the public comparing the quality of my efforts and the style of the older cartoonist. The differences were very pronounced in our style, approach to a theme, sense of humour and draftsmanship. I never used our gods, demons or folk tales to illustrate any current political events. Nor did I make politicians look like cows or donkeys or convert a male with fierce moustaches into a coy saree-clad woman. I dealt with satirical concepts strictly on the familiar level of everyday life. I followed the standard rules of perspective, drapery and anatomy; when I caricatured a personality I exercised controlled distortion. This appealed to the class of readers with sophisticated taste.

But there were many readers owing allegiance to the older cartoonist who had been a national figure. They felt that my exhibition in the capital was presumptuous.

This opinion was confirmed by a prominent elderly member of the Congress party who spelt it out unambiguously. I took her round the gallery with all the respect and deference due to her position and age. I could not guess what she thought of my cartoons because she kept a straight face during the half hour she spent in the gallery. But before she left she said, 'You should not have displayed your work in Delhi. If you think you can overshadow our veteran cartoonist who is famous and experienced and whom we all simply adore, you are thoroughly mistaken, young man . . .'

After returning to Bombay I began my usual routine, leading the life of a squirrel in a wheel cage. I would be at the drawing board in the office exactly at 8.30 in the morning, reading and concentrating on news items, political analyses, editorial commentaries, opinions, spending the time tormenting myself, waiting hopelessly for the muse of satire to oblige me with an idea for the next day's cartoon before the deadline. When the idea did at last dawn, the rest of the work was comparatively easy. It was like shooting a movie—choosing a suitable setting, selecting the characters, compressing the script into a brief caption. I might visualize a mountain cliff with someone like Nehru hanging from it precariously. It could be a cage with the rulers inside and the tiger of the black market, crime, scarcity, stalking freely outside. Or I might conceive of a huge limousine with all the reigning political stalwarts seated comfortably inside but no one to take the driver's seat. I swiftly sketched the idea in pencil, inked it, wrote the caption and added final details. By then I would have put in six hours of continuous work. Mentally and physically exhausted, I would go home. But the sense of fulfilment and creative satisfaction would be immense.

Diversion from such a light, self-imposed schedule was meeting friends in the evening or attending parties. But people were so pre-occupied with political events that once again the conversation would be a boring repetition of the news in the morning paper. I needed something different to keep my mind off politics and politicians.

A solution to my inflexible routine presented itself one day in the shape of a old rusted timepiece. I came by it accidentally while rummaging through a box of junk into which I had dumped nails, nuts and bolts, hammers, screwdrivers and other such items. Among these I found the discarded clock gathering rust and decaying. It was a famous Smith alarm, made in England. It had stopped many years ago at ten minutes to ten. I immediately extricated it and began to work on it. With the help of some oil, petrol and a screwdriver, I took it apart. I collected all the springs, screws and wheels in a heap and cleaned each part meticulously. I never noticed the time pass! I had spent nearly three hours on the job. I felt relaxed and refreshed. I wanted to put all the parts back in their places and make the clock work.

I have always had a fascination for machinery. I never missed a chance to visit an industrial plant! When I was in Germany I requested my host, much to his amazement, to take me to the Mercedes Benz factory. In the US I visited General Electric, and Toyota and Sony in Japan. In China I wandered in the coal mining area looking at all the earth-moving, digging and pounding machines. In our own country, I have spent time in places such as textile mills, food processing plants, Tata iron and steel works.

At home I was a sort of handyman who replaced washers in leaky taps, mended water pipes, replaced fuses, repaired an electric iron, connected valves in pressure cookers. Now I worked on the Smith alarm clock with undivided attention after returning from the office, having dealt with Govind Vallabh Pant, Vallabbhai Patel, Jayaprakash Narain, the finance minister, the food minster etc. Finally after a week I succeeded in making the clock tick again!

Then I found another disused clock. I repaired that too. But it was so badly damaged I had to buy balance wheels, hairsprings and other intricate items from a regular clock repairer.

When my friends learnt that I repaired clocks they collected their old broken ones and brought them to me for repair. But between my freelance work and official travels I took so long to repair one that the people who gave me the clocks gave up all hopes of getting them back and finally forgot about them.

Meanwhile I myself was becoming tired of dismantling, oiling and reassembling clocks. At the end of two years I started showing impatience with the tools, lost my temper with clocks that obstinately behaved unpunctually after repairs.

Slowly this diversion dropped out of my life. But the urge to do something different after coming back home from the office continued. So I began to think of writing. But somehow my brother's dominant image as a reputed writer made me self-conscious and shy. Still, I attempted a few short stories, essays and travelogues. These were published in the *Illustrated Weekly*.

It was about this time that I found the famous British cartoonist David Low sitting in my office when I entered one morning. His brief visit elevated my status in the *Times* office. On the strength of it I suggested to the editor that I would benefit professionally if I was sent to England for a brief trip to meet the cartoonists there and exchange views. The management was most unexpectedly favourable to the proposal recommended by the editor. Soon the funds were sanctioned, and letters despatched to the London office of the *Times of India*, requesting that I be given all possible assistance while I was there.

The editor was also good enough to write more than a dozen letters of introduction to various editors of London newspapers. All the letters, of course, were identical except the starting which began 'Dear Charles' or 'Dear Frank', or 'Dear Jim' . . . 'This is to introduce our *Times of India* cartoonist who is going on a businessman's holiday to England. His work is widely appreciated in India and many consider him the best political cartoonist in the country. I should be much obliged if you give him any help he may need . . .' etc.

Some relatives who had studied in Oxford, or Cambridge, or London School of Economics also provided letters of introduction to their friends in London. I had a few friends who had emigrated to England. I wrote and told them when I was arriving, and asked them to guide me through London till I settled down.

I did not have the haziest idea of London, nor did I plan where I was going to stay. I did not know which direction I should take after I stepped out of the aircraft. But I went about briskly arranging for my passport and visas for the countries I hoped to visit. Then I bought some warm clothes, borrowed an overcoat from a friend and booked my air passage to England. I was all set to take off.

On the day of departure, a large group of friends and relatives gathered at the airport to see me off. They stood around advising me to be careful with my passport and traveller's cheques. They admired me in my newly tailored dark suit, corrected the knot in my tie, pulled my leg, joked and asked me over and over to drop a line about my safe arrival at London. They bought magazines and books for me to read during the journey and thrust them into my arms which were already loaded with my overcoat, sweater and handbag.

After a few hours of being airborne, I began to find the journey tedious and endless. The darkness outside and the steady drone of the plane left me neither wakeful nor sleepy. I saw uninteresting faces sitting alongside me. I tried to read, but could not. I went on staring at the pattern of upholstery of the seat in front of me, till I dozed off. I woke up to the clinking of glasses and found that drinks were being served. I ordered mine, had my food and went off to sleep again. I lost track of time and repeated this order every time I woke till the plane showed signs of descending. Finally we landed at Heathrow.

It was drizzling. The arrival sector soon became desolate, all the passengers having found their way out at various exits. I was left alone clutching my suitcase. I saw some airport buses lined up, and people struggling on board with their baggage. I could not see a single smiling face. Everyone looked grim, hooded uniformly in dark clothes, like creatures in limbo. I failed to summon the courage to ask anyone for directions. If I took the bus which said Waterloo

Terminal, where should I go, I questioned myself.

A whole world of depression enveloped me. I wondered how was I to spend so many months in that ambience! Just as I was despairing, I suddenly saw an old friend leaning against a wall under a dull lamplight. I had vaguely written to this soul as I had done to a few others, but I never expected him to be there to receive me!

He came running and gave me a warm hug. He asked if I had seen his note. He went into the terminus and plucked a letter from a notice board. He had left directions about where he would be waiting for me after I disembarked. He called me a country bumpkin.

He was brimming with cheer and made many enquiries about people back home. I could not match his energy and enthusiasm as I was suffering from the combined effects of jetlag, insufficient food and a hangover.

We both got into a taxi. As I settled down he startled me by suddenly barking at the driver; 'Camden Town!' showing off a great deal of British style of speaking and a lot of accent.

He took me to his flat, lugging my suitcase up the stairs. It was a small place consisting of a bedroom, sitting room and kitchenette. He noticed that I was tired and sleepy. He converted the sofa into a cosy, warm bed and suggested that I retire.

The next morning he took me around and taught me how to get into the bus or tube, and how to find my way to various places I wanted to visit. He took me to the India Club where we had a regular Indian lunch; then he showed me my office in Albemarle Street off Piccadilly. He gave quite a bit of advice, hints and tips to help me cope with the English eccentricities and habits.

As we were returning home I wanted to find a hotel I could move into. I was not inclined to prolong my makeshift arrangement as a guest in my friend's flat for the rest of my stay in London.

But luckily, thanks to him, in a couple of days he found me a similar apartment in the same building, just opposite his own door at three pounds a week.

When I started living in the flat I used to leave the rent on the mantelpiece every Monday before I left for the office and when I returned at night I found a stamped receipt in its place. I never saw the person who collected the rent even once during my stay. Similarly, the old lady who dusted and cleaned the flat collected her wages from the mantelpiece.

The flat was compact, comfortable and neat, with a gas-ring in the kitchenette which worked when a coin was dropped into a slot next to it. The rear window of my room framed a landscape of a majestically rising Hampstead Heath. The whole character of the place fitted my idea of living in London. I made it my home till I returned to India.

I bought two maps; one showing bus routes of London and another routes of tube trains. Armed with these I reached my office at Albemarle Street effortlessly. I was accommodated in our London correspondent's room and given a table, chair and telephone. The small group of staff members gathered round and each member was introduced to me.

I was asked the purpose of my visit to London. I produced the list of personalities I intended to meet and caricature and rolled off the names—David Low, Graham Greene, Bertrand Russell, J.B. Priestley, T.S. Eliot. On hearing the list all the eyebrows went up indicating I was being presumptuous and naïve. These individuals were not easily accessible, particularly to a cartoonist from India, of all people! Of course, they did not openly mention it but it was in the air and I could sense it. The staff looked at each other as if I had already failed in my ambitious mission. They sat in silence looking at each other. However I broke the awkward silence by requesting them to get me the telephone numbers and addresses of the people on my list which they did, I thought, on compassionate grounds.

My plan was to meet the personalities methodically, one by one; finish the caricature, taking a week; mail it to Bombay, and then go on to the next. This way I would complete my plan in six weeks. Then I would go sightseeing and visiting places of interest.

Thus with this neat schedule in hand, I rang up the first person on the list, David Low. I was all excited and tense as the phone rang. I composed the words as it went on ringing, 'Hello Mr Low, remember me? . . . I'm Laxman. We met in Bombay last year.' But the phone went on ringing till I saw, in my mind's eye, empty rooms echoing with the ring of the telephone. I tried once more an hour later, then again in the afternoon, in the evening and at night, with mounting obsession.

I suffered the disappointment silently and wondered if my colleagues at the office were not, after all, right in thinking that I over-rated myself as a famous cartoonist from India and believed that all doors would open at the mention of my name.

Then I went on to the next person on the list, Graham Greene. Without hope I rang up. A lady answered. I identified myself and said I wished to see the famous writer. She replied that she would certainly convey my message after Greene returned from holiday in the south of France.

I realized I had landed in London at a bad time; everyone was on holiday.

To justify my presence in London I started a feature called 'Our Cartoonist Abroad' for the *Times of India*. I depicted the familiar figure of the Common Man mixing with the London crowds and observing the British way of life. After I had exhausted this theme I decided to go on a sightseeing tour. I booked my seat in buses and trains. I covered all the art galleries, museums, castles, palaces, parks, gardens. I journeyed out of London to visit Oxford, Cambridge, Stratford, Brighton, Kent, Dover.

After I had exhausted all the tourist spots I started to frequent the Artists and Writers Club in which I was enrolled as a member. Here I made friends with writers, actors and artists. On the whole I was having a great time. But that was not my purpose in London. The thought that I had not yet succeeded in meeting even a single eminent writer was weighing on my mind. I had a suspicion that the people in my office were laughing up their sleeves at my plight.

When I could not bear it any longer I rang up Graham Greene once more. His secretary this time put me on, at last, to him. He was delighted and asked me to come over to his place at once if I was free. He was staying in Albany Court, just a few minutes walk from our office. I left quietly without telling anyone. I was also happy that I was visiting a place where Lord Byron had once lived when he was in London.

Graham Greene was already at the door as I came up the stairs. He went on staring at me. 'Does Narayan look like you?' he asked. He had been friends with my brother for several years but their contact had been only through letters; they had not seen each other. It was another six years before they really got to meet each other. Greene led me to the sitting room and moved about with slow grace, collecting two glasses and a bottle of scotch from the bar. It was only eleven o'clock in the morning and I could never drink before sundown. But at that moment I was not inclined to refuse.

He was very curious about Narayan and asked many questions about his habits, tastes and methods of work. Then the topic turned to Narayan's novels and various characters that my brother had portrayed. As we talked I studied Greene's face, taking note of the many folds, furrows and creases which kept appearing and vanishing alternately registering his emotions.

A few days later I worked on the caricature in colour. The office staff craned their necks, standing behind my chair to get a glimpse of what I was painting. Our correspondent was surprised that I had succeeded in my mission and asked many questions about Greene, his apartment, our conversation. I mailed the caricature to the *Illustrated Weekly*. It was the first sketch to appear in the series, 'Personalities'.

Meanwhile I had become a familiar figure at the bar and dining room of the India Club. In the evenings it was usually crowded with visiting Indian businessmen, non-resident Indians, Indian journalists and some staff members of our Indian High Commission. All these people starved of spicy Indian food converged on the India Club in the evening. I used to invite some of my Fleet Street friends for drinks and a typical south Indian meal.

One Saturday after an enjoyable evening with friends I had my dinner and left for my apartment at Hampstead. On the way I picked up a bottle of brandy for a nightcap. After all the next day was Sunday, and I could lie abed as long as I wanted.

In the foyer of the apartment I was looking in the mailbox for letters when I noticed a person studying some prints of British landscapes hung on the walls. His white teeth flashed brightly against the soft dusky colour of his complexion as he introduced himself. He was from the West Indies. He had arrived only that morning. He was going to be in London for two months studying something under the sponsorship of the British Railways. He had taken lodgings in the same building. He seemed a cultivated, friendly type and I was moved to invite him for a drink in my room. Seated comfortably, we talked for hours, stopping only to refill our glasses. We discussed our countries, habits, culture, people, religion, parents, ancestors, beliefs, theories, and so on.

When I woke the next day I could not recall when we had parted company. I bathed and dressed and stepped out to have my brunch. I found the streets unusually crowded for a Sunday. The shops were open. There was heavy traffic on the road. The expressions on the faces of hurrying pedestrians seemed concerned and purposeful. I took a stroll on Hampstead Heath as I usually did on Sundays, to view the London skyline, the silhouettes of St. Paul's Cathedral, London Bridge, Westminister. The Heath was deserted. There were no picnickers and holiday-makers. I returned to my room much puzzled. On the way I stopped at a railway station bearing the picturesque name of Gospel Oak, and bought a copy of the daily newspaper. My eyes skimmed the headlines and came to rest on the date, sending a shock wave through me. It was not Sunday but Monday! I had slept the whole of Sunday! One whole day of my life had gone without my knowing!

When I went to the office on Tuesday a letter from J.B. Priestley awaited me. Having read his books *The Good Companions*, *Angel Pavement* and *Midnight in a Desert*, not to mention Priestley's famous Time plays, I had dashed off a letter to him at the address of his publishers asking for an appointment. This letter was his reply inviting me to tea at his apartment at Albany Court.

I found Priestley puckish. He bounced about the drawing room, hardly sitting down for a moment, carrying his rotund heavy self with surprising nimbleness. He declared that he was essentially a humorous writer and wished that I would portray him as such. He was pleased with the few quick sketches I made as I talked about the characters in his novels. By the time I left I had the feeling I was with one of his creations in *The Good Companions*.

Encouraged by this encounter, I boldly rang up T.S. Eliot at the office of Faber & Faber. I knew it was a very rash move. I had heard about Eliot's temperament and braced myself to face the brush-off. His secretary answered. Through the voice I could visualize the programmed middle-aged secretary in a grey cardigan—'Mr Eliot does not receive calls. Mr Eliot does not receive visitors. Mr Eliot does not give interviews either,' she said over-politely.

Soon, other diversions blotted out the frustrating experience. My cartoonist friends frequently asked me to show them my work. So I sometimes carried a bundle of my political cartoons and coloured caricatures. One day I called on David Low to make his caricature over a cup of tea at his flat. After the meeting I left for the India Club to have my dinner. The place was crowded. People were going in and out. A cocktail party was in full swing. The guests overflowed from the main hall into other rooms. They were clutching their glasses and talking in low deferential tones—a rather unusual trait generally for the guests at the India Club. I stood at the outer ring of the crowd, trying to locate the centre of attraction.

The secretary of the club spotted me and invited me to join the party. V.K. Krishna Menon was standing in the middle of what seemed a charmed circle of listeners. He was holding forth, swinging his walking stick, cutting and thrusting the air to illustrate, perhaps, his performance in the UN General Assembly. The secretary held on to my elbow propelling me towards Menon to introduce me to him. I quickly shoved my bundle of cartoons behind a chair and reluctantly let myself be introduced. I had done several cartoons of him in his many roles as a prominent player in Indian politics. Now he was our roving Ambassador, and like some dark wasp flitted from capital to capital—Paris, Geneva, New York, Washington, Moscow, New Delhi, Prague, and so on. I had done a colour caricature of him for the *Weekly*, showing him carrying two suitcases plastered with names of various capitals of the world. This cartoon was in the bundle I had brought along.

As a rule I avoided meeting politicians. In my professional life I had learnt that when a politician congratualated me on my cartoon of the day and thumped me on the back saying I was a genius, he had just seen a nasty cartoon about his political enemy in the opposition or in his own party. On the other hand if a politician pumped my hand with warm and generous admiration for a cartoon in which I had ridiculed him, he was bound to start quietly telling me in a roundabout way that I lacked political judgement, and end up teaching me how to draw cartoons.

Finally the secretary succeeded in penetrating the crowd encircling Menon. He smiled and shook my hand warmly, and resumed addressing the audience where he had left off when I caused the interruption. Suddenly we noticed a disturbance at the other end of the room. Menon stopped his narration and frowned. He tried to continue, but his listeners were not paying him their undivided attention any more, and began to slink away towards the source of the noise. I was horrified when I saw that someone had taken the colour caricature of Menon from the bundle of cartoons I had left behind a chair. It was being passed on from hand to hand with great glee and uproarious comments.

Giggles and guffaws filled the hall. I knew Menon would not like it. I helplessly watched the caricature finally landing in the hands of Menon. He looked at the caricature without a smile. The crowd waited with bated breath for the reaction of a man who was internationally notorious for his quick temper and sharp tongue. But I already knew what he would say, and sure enough he said it: 'But this does not look like me!' Actually my caricature looked more like him than he himself did! It was acclaimed as one of my best efforts. In order to dispel the tension the cartoon seemed to have created, I said, 'What about autographing it, sir? I shall treasure it.'

For a moment he appeared uncertain, then remarked as if his voice had the seal of authority on it, 'One never autographs one's caricature. It is not done, young man.'

'But, Nehru, Patel, Azad, C.R., Pant, . . .' I mumbled. Then he took out his pen, saying, 'I can give you my autograph on a separate piece of paper but definitely not on that caricature.' I immediately replied, 'No thank you, sir. The autograph has no value to me unless it is on the caricature I have made.'

My failure to meet T.S. Eliot was bothering me a grat deal. Back in India my colleagues were anxiously waiting for my colour caricature of this celebrity. I was fighting shy of telling them that the poet seemed to live in a fortress, and that I had been asked to keep off.

At this time Graham Greene called me over for a drink one evening. We talked about travels in India, its culture, Gandhi, Nehru, politics and various other subjects. Somehow the topic turned to astrology, palmistry, horoscopes. I spoke as best as I could, managing with the little I knew about these matters. Before I left that evening, Greene made a strange request. He wrote down his date and year of birth and asked me to have his horoscope cast when I returned to India, and to send him the chart. I readily agreed. He said if there was anything I wanted he would try and help me. I hesitated for a moment, then decided that this could be my last chance. I mentioned my disappointment with T.S. Eliot. Greene said he was sorry to hear that, and quietly added, 'I will fix an appointment for you.' He went in to make a phone call even as I was leaving.

A couple of days later I was sitting with Eliot in his study, feeling like a gatecrasher and a spoilt brat. He uttered some obvious pleasantries but was mostly silent. As I began to make rough sketches of his tall figure, large nose and dreamy eyes, I told him about a poet I had met in London, who claimed that he knew Eliot so well that Eliot had written an introduction to a collection of that man's poems, currently in press. When I mentioned the individual's name, Eliot raised his eyebrows and said he had neither heard of the poet, nor had he written a foreword to any such book! Then he sat still, as if posing for an oil portrait. I made an elaborate pencil study of him. When I finished I held it out for him to autograph. He continued to sit without stirring. I had to clear my throat loudly, for he had gone to sleep. He woke up with a start and looked apologetic. He gazed at my drawing with amusement and signed it cheerfully.

I am grateful to Graham Greene for his help. But even today I feel deep guilt and shame when I think of him. Unaccountably, I failed to keep the promise I had made that I would get his horoscope cast!

I had won a victory of sorts getting at Eliot. Next on my list was Bertrand Russell. I was prepared to be cold-shouldered by him. Without a sense of disappointment because it would be more than made up my by the chance to attend Britain's Labour Party conference at Scarborough in Yorkshire, to which I had just been invited. There I would have the opportunity to study the leading politicians at close quarters, and at one sweep caricature Atlee, Bevan, Gaitskell, Wilson, Morrison and many others.

Just before leaving for Scarborough I phoned Bertrand Russell without any expectations. I was not sure, in the first place, how to address him if at all he condescended to pick up the phone. Should I call him Sir Bertrand, or Earl Russell, or Lord Honourable . . . or just plain Mr Bertrand Russell? However when the phone rang, someone picked it up. I introduced myself as a cartoonist from India, and said I would like to meet 'Russell', slurring over the title part. The voice answered, 'Hullo, I am Bertrand Russell here, when do you wish to come?' I was staggered, having suffered the tedium of chasing other celebrities! He went on, 'Can you come now?' I could not say whether I could or could not—this was too unexpected. I was thoroughly confused! While I was struggling for a reply, his lordship's voice asked, 'Where are you speaking from? Oh, Albemarle Street, Piccadilly? Good! Now listen—just take a walk down from your office to Green Park station. Take the tube. Get off at Earl's Court and cross over to the Green Line and take the one going to Richmond. And take care you don't get into one going to Hounslow West or Wimbledon. When you come to Richmond any taxi driver will bring you to my house. Are you coming now?' I had no choice but to say 'yes', and follow his instructions to reach his place.

Richmond had a tiny station. I was almost the only one to get off the train, which in a second shot off like a bullet gathering speed and disappeared.

Outside I saw a couple of taxis. The drivers were reading the newspapers as usual. The whole place looked like a picture postcard, with typical timber-framed brick cottages with tiled red roofs, flowering trees, narrow cobbled side lanes. I got into a taxi, and as the driver started the car, I mentioned where I wanted to be taken. He turned towards me and smiled. He took a curve along the fencing of a park, and hardly had he changed from first to second gear when he stopped and said, 'There it is . . .' pointing to a picturesque cottage. It had a generous cluster of trees, flower beds and ivy creepers over the walls. Sir Bertrand stood by the white wicket gate, with a smile that also held a pipe firmly.

From the moment we sat down in his study it was one long entertainment for me. We got on as if we had known each other for ages. The man was full of sparkling wit, anecdotes and aphorisms. We discussed Gandhi, non-violence, Hitler, Nehru, the atom bomb, the cruelty that man inflicted on man, the triumph of good over evil and evil over good alternating down the ages, which was the stuff of human history. Thus we talked freely in a philosophical mood, neither being conscious of our intellectual status. For an ordinary person like me, who was no devotee of the *Principia Mathematica*, he put me at ease and made me forget I was conversing with one of the world's greatest philosophers and mathematicians.

'You know, the short story form is the best way to convey an idea. I just discovered this,' he said. Then he narrated several stories to make his point. Actually I had illustrated some of his short stories published in the *Times of India*. I had brought along the illustration I had made for 'The Doctor and the Devil'. He was very pleased, and autographed it along with a pencil portrait I had made of him while we talked.

I was absolutely pleased with the unhurried long session I had with him and started gathering my things to depart. He made no attempt to get up and see me off. He started to stuff his pipe in a leisurely manner and said, 'You Indians discovered nothing!' I was taken aback by the sudden, jarring and uncalled-for rude remark! I wondered where I had erred in my conduct to provoke him to say such a nasty thing. I did not know how to react to the barbarous assault on our nation, race, heritage, culture. He repeated,

'Absolutely nothing!' observing me with his smiling eyes, lips clutching around his pipe in his patent style. What devil had possessed this man, I raved within, returning to my seat, determined to challenge him. But I could not think of a single point at that moment to defend myself. I found the sofa I sat on too far away to target him properly. So I moved up and sat on the carpet near him. With controlled vehemence I said, 'That is not a fair observation to make, Mr Russell . . .' But he repeated, 'Indians discovered absolutely nothing . . .' I raised my voice and retorted, 'What about chess? Who discovered that? Philosophical concepts . . . literature, classics,' I went on hurling at him blindly whatever came to my mind.

Mischief twinkled in his keen blue eyes as he said, 'Calm down, young man. I am paying you people a great compliment. The concept of Zero is a great mathematical discovery and the credit goes entirely to Indian thinkers! I am a great admirer of Indian thought . . .' Smiling triumphantly, his ruffled shock of white hair in a frozen explosion over his head, he looked like a cockatoo in a devilish mood. I have never met a man who was so great and yet so utterly charming!

I went to Scarborough in a car accompanied by a few other journalists. We reached the outskirts of London, and entered tiny townships with narrow cobbled lanes having signboards of pubs on either side. I wondered what inspired the owners to give their establishments names like: 'The Ram', 'The Pinewood', 'The Lion', 'The Falcon', with appropriate figures colourfully painted on the signboards. I saw old patrons hobbling in and out of the pubs. The scenes flashed past before I could fully absorb the details for my sketch book. But soon we entered another lane with identical fixtures. Gradually the villages and towns were left behind, and we emerged into an area with vast green meadows spread like an undulating carpet on either side.

The whole journey was a visual delight—distant clusters of trees on the arced hump of the horizon, old weather-beaten churches, wooden fences, fleecy flocks of sheep crossing the road, straw-thatched humble huts, acres of heather-covered moorlands. All these were somehow familiar sights. They had remained till now just images formed in the mind when reading English classics, poetry, plays, novels, short stories over the years.

While musing thus, I was distracted by an incongruous blackboard on the side of the road, conspicuously placed to catch our attention. 'TEA' was written on it in bold letters. An arrow pointed to a nearby cottage.

We stopped the car and trooped into the house. An old lady was sitting in a rocking chair, knitting—once again a sight so typical of the illustrations by John Tenniel for Dickens's stories.

She greeted us warmly, asked us to sit down. She herself sat down for a few seconds, then went in and brought us pots of hot tea and biscuits. She moved about like a perfect hostess, enquiring about what we needed, offering more tea and generally talking about the weather, the garden, the flowers.

Thoroughly refreshed, we took leave of her, expressing our thanks. The commercial aspect of her hospitality was so elegantly concealed. We paid for the tea, of course, dropping the money into a tray discreetly placed behind a curtain near the door.

As we resumed the journey we saw quite a few placards and signboards by the road, announcing 'TEA'.

*

Finally we arrived at Scarborough. The hotel we were booked in was beautifully located, overlooking the sea with a sandy shore in front. The lobby was big and crowded with delegates who had arrived for the conference. After completing the formalities at the desk I collected the key and went to my room. I washed, changed my clothes and parted the curtains of the window to peep out at the landscape. It was dark, but I could discern rugged sloping rocks and the waves crashing against them.

I went down to join my friends. They were already comfortably seated with glasses in their grips. I collected my drink and surveyed the vast gathering, trying to spot known faces. Bevan with his tall bulk was the only one I could see. At that moment someone touched my shoulders and said, 'Hello!' His voice was hardly audible in the surrounding din and chatter. I jumped out of my seat when I saw who he was. It was David Low again! We shook hands and I invited him to join us. But he pointed to someone at the far end of the hall, excused himself and moved away. Of course, my friends had no clue as to who he was. When I told them they were excited. One of the correspondents for an Indian paper was so overcome that he stood up and shouted, much to my embarrassment, 'Low, hello there Low, come and have a drink!' Low turned round, conveyed through lip movement—sorry it had to be another time, and disappeared into the crowd.

The Labour conference was to begin at nine the next morning. I got up early and stepped out of the room, fresh after a good night's sleep and a bath. The dining room was already full of delegates guzzling breakfast. As I was looking for a place to sit, I saw Clement Atlee. Next to him sat Vicky, another famous cartoonist I used to meet in the Artists and Writers Club in London. There were two others seated next to Atlee—a portly gentleman with a beard, and a rather thin young man. After being introduced to them I sat down and began to make mental notes of Atlee's features and mannerisms.

The bearded man was from East Pakistan (now Bangladesh), and spoke in a language none of us could understand, except his thin companion. Each time the Pakistani said something, we all turned to the thin fellow who was his official interpreter. The subject under discussion when I joined them was the American wheat supplied to East Pakistan. It was rotten and unfit for consumption. We all nodded in sympathy and made anti-American noises, showing our outrage and indignation. Again the Pakistani uttered something and the young translator followed up immediately, 'Even donkeys won't eat! That bad! We have self-respect, sir! We starve and perish. But not eat that. Never!' After relaying his anger he resumed his normal composure. The bearded man who so far had sat in dignified silence, continued the story in a slow rumbling tone without gestures, without emotion. As he finished, the young chap remarked ferociously, 'There was no grain. It was a shipload of dust and worms to be thrown into the Bay of Bengal.'

We expressed our shock in various ways, and prepared to leave for the conference hall. It was located about half a kilometre from the hotel, a pleasant walk in the sand towards the beach. I sidled up to Atlee and requested for his autograph when the caricature was completed. 'Of course. Please leave it with the receptionist. I will autograph it and have it delivered to your room.' Coincidentally, my room was just next to his.

I sat in the conference hall's press enclosure. The delegates were in a jolly mood and moved about in all directions, greeting each other, joking and laughing. Suddenly silence fell. The meeting came to order.

One after another the party leaders began to make their speeches. Their theatrical stance, hands in trouser pockets, nonchalant thumbs tucked into the armpits, seemed to be posing just for my benefit to sketch which I did abundantly.

But I could not make out what the speakers were saying, however much I tried. Their pronunciation was different from what they sounded like when met individually. It looked as if they were striking a deliberate pose and putting on acts to impress the audience.

After a while I got bored and slipped out. It was nearing lunch time. I headed for the hotel. I had a beer and lunch and went up to my room to start working on Atlee's caricature.

I completed it towards evening, taking help from the rough sketches I had made of his prominent features and other particular aspects of his personality. But I had always found that such notes and realistic photographic details are not much help in caricaturing a face—without making it look grotesque, which is popularly mistaken for caricature. The art of ideal caricature is to bring out the essence of a personality through credible exaggeration.

In my experience, the image of a person that occurs in

one's memory is of great help. The prominence of a rather large nose or a pair of luxuriant bushy eyebrows or a shiny bald pate or a double chin seem important in reality for caricature. But a face appears in one's memory without light or shade or physical distance in space. That is what is required to understand the essence of a personality.

So I sat in my room, recalling the face of Atlee over and over till I distilled it as a caricature on a sheet of paper. I put the drawing in an envelope and handed it over to the receptionist, as Atlee had suggested.

It was cocktail hour, but I found the lounge barely crowded. I joined the group I had sat with in the morning, and spent the evening quietly.

Next morning I was again at the conference. This time I made sketches of Bevan, Gaitskill and Morrison.

In the evening I went for a walk by myself. The cottages and houses on either side of the street were a gloomy uniform grey. The windows were shut and lace curtains were drawn over them. The few occupants who peeped out looked ancient, and seemed startled at the sight of a stranger. They did not seem to have moved for generations beyond the grocery shop, the butcher, the pub and occasionally the sea front.

Contemplating on these impressions, I proceeded towards my hotel. I missed India, though the ruminating cows right in the middle of the road, the pyramids of garbage, the stink, the crowds, the perpetual state of pandemonium were constant irritations. My thoughts were interrupted by a board I saw nailed to the gate of a cottage—*Emmary Young, astrologer, palmist, numerologist. Consultancy hours from 9 a.m. to 12 p.m. From 4 p.m. to 6.30 p.m. All consultations will be kept strictly confidential.* It was a welcome comic touch in a sombre, depressing atmosphere.

I collected my room key and went up, expecting an envelope from Atlee. But I was disappointed. I did not know where and how to contact this man! He had vanished from sight since I saw him on the first day. He returned late at night after the conference and left the hotel early in the morning. I felt it was rather delicate to ask him on the phone. Nor did I want to leave a note at the lobby desk. Time was running out. The conference was coming to an end and everyone was leaving at various points of time the next day.

I went down to the lounge hoping to meet someone who would help. The lights were dimmed and small groups sat huddled, conversing in low tones. I sat in an isolated corner and sipped my drink, expecting a familiar face to turn up. Even those with whom I was to return to London the following day were nowhere around. After dinner I returned to my room and read till late into the night, hoping there would be a call from Atlee. After some time I lost all hope of retrieving my caricature. I switched off the light and drifted into sleep.

The next morning we were returning to London after breakfast. So I took my time getting up. I had an unhurried bath, dressed and went down for breakfast. As I was about to step out of the room, I saw a brown envelope pushed under the door. Good old Atlee, at last! He had kept his word and had returned the caricature autographed with his compliments! I wanted to thank him but he had already checked out of the hotel very early in the morning.

After returning to London, I began to pack for my homeward journey after nearly six months in England. I had arrived with just one suitcase and a handbag. Now these had multiplied into four odd-shaped packages. I had bought suit material, shoes, any number of ties, socks, pants and shirts which carried famous brand-names. There were also items listed by friends and relatives, apart from kitchen gadgets for my household. I was also obliged to carry gifts for near and dear ones and toys for their kids. The last few days in London were spent hopping from shop to shop, checking my lists and trying to cram all the items into whatever space was available in my boxes.

I had booked my passage to India via Paris, Geneva and Rome, with halts of a couple of days in each place. I took leave of the staff at the office, wined and dined with friends bidding them good-bye, and said farewell to those I knew at India Club and at the Artists and Writers Club and friends in Fleet Street. Somehow after this hectic activity, a day before my departure, which was a Sunday, I was left all alone without anything to do. I wandered aimlessly around Piccadilly Circus, entered Green Park and moved on to Hyde Park. I walked along the Serpentine, watched people fishing, and children launching paper boats. A man was issuing tickets for rides near the boathouse. People were rowing to and from a short jetty. At that time some strange attraction impelled me towards the window to buy a ticket. Here I was who never was adventurous or had ventured into water except for a bath safely in a bathroom. But now I could not believe myself—I was hiring a boat!

I sat in the boat clutching the oars. The man who sold tickets disappeared into the boathouse after giving me a push. I drifted away from the shore. I saw the boathouse and the people standing around getting smaller and smaller. I had never held an oar in my hand and did not know how to operate it to move forward. However I gripped the oars firmly and moved them forward and backward. The boat turned round and round without going in any direction. I looked for the boathouse with the idea of abandoning my adventure. But it was nowhere to be seen. Without my realizing it, the boat had drifted far away from the shore, into the middle of the lake. Carried by the current, I suddenly found myself drifting under the span of a bridge. I tried to paddle again towards the boathouse, but the boat wobbled dangerously, threatening to toss me overboard. I heard someone shout, 'Watch out!' I had just missed ramming into a passing boat. The chap was rowing vigorously. I watched the way he was working the oars. I managed to follow it. Soon I was able to recover and clumsily move forward. It look me hours to crawl towards the boathouse, gritting my teeth against the pain in my shoulders. My palms were burning—the skin on them had peeled off from rubbing against the oars. Finally I docked at the boathouse. The ticket seller looked at his watch and glared at me. He must have watched my antics on the Serpentine through the window of the boathouse!

In Paris I was a typical tourist—went up the Eiffel Tower, visited the famous Notre Dame Cathedral, and spent most of the day inside art galleries. In the evenings I watched striptease shows at night clubs, and returned to the hotel late at night after an indifferent vegetarian dinner and plenty of French wine.

After the hectic tour of Paris I left for Geneva. I found it extremely pretty but dull, like a spiritless picture postcard. With my sketchbook in hand I wandered around looking for subjects to draw, as I always did wherever I went. I hardly observed anything that stirred my whimsical sense to record. Everything seemed too idyllic and contrived! Lake Geneva reflected the surrounding mountains as if made to order. There were flowering trees, rich homes arranged neatly on the hillsides, immaculate flower beds everywhere, fountains playing in the middle of the city. There were no maimed statues of ancient heroes, historical fortresses in ruins or weather-beaten churches. The only monument I saw was that of William Tell, the ace archer who shot an apple balanced on his little son's head with an arrow.

The Swiss were pink-cheeked and healthy and seemed to have been produced out of a standard mould. I could not bring myself to sketch those stereotyped faces. I actually saw a man prop a green ladder against an apple tree in the middle of a deep green lawn. He went up the ladder, gleefully plucked succulent blood-red apples and dropped them on the lawn. Then he collected them in a basket and walked away, beaming with satisfaction. I was not inspired to sketch that scene. It was like a stage set for a play. I needed a certain ruggedness, crooked lines, broken dry twigs, disorder, and discoloration in the landscape, unshaven faces, ill-fitting pants!

Geneva was good for holding international conferences and transacting banking business—not a place for one who looked for oddities in human situations, I concluded as I left for Rome.

Arriving there was like entering an immense open-air museum of marble arches, colossal statues, ruined amphitheatres. Flights of stone steps led to various levels of houses, to churches and narrow alleys and bridges. Here I encountered a different kind of problem from what I had faced in Switzerland. I found objects to sketch in every direction I turned; people with high cheekbones, deep-set eyes, aquiline noses, children in cobbled squares gambolling with hundreds of fluttering pigeons, fat women framed in the windows of their ancient dwellings watching the goings-on in the crowded street below, houses with gardens, creepers and wrought-iron balconies in which one could effortlessly conjure up Juliet awaiting Romeo.

Then, of course, the rich fare offered in the Vatican, Michaelangelo's marble statues, and his magnificent murals in the Sistine Chapel.

I had a most eerie experience while going about enjoying the aesthetic beauty of all these. I was taken to visit the catacombs. A tall thin priest dressed in a brown surplice led the way into an underground tunnel which became narrower and darker as we proceeded. He lit a four-foot candle and held it aloft as we walked. At one point I was horrified to find gruesomely near my face, human skeletons—adults and children—embedded in hollows scooped in the cave's mud walls. There were hundreds of them as we went deeper and deeper into the tunnel.

lived in Switzerland. I found objects to sketch in every direction I turned: people with high cheekbones, deep-set eyes, aquiline noses; children in cobbled squares consorting with multitudes of fluttering pigeons; old women framed in the windows of their ancient dwellings watching the goings on in the crowded street below; houses with gardens, balconies and wrought-iron balconies in which one could effortlessly imagine a Juliet awaiting Romeo.

Then of course the rich fare offered in the Vatican, Michelangelo's marble statues, and his magnificent murals in the Sistine Chapel.

I had a more eerie experience while going about enjoying the luminous beauty of it all. I was taken to visit the catacombs. A tall thin priest dressed in a brown surplice led the way into an underground tunnel which became narrower and darker as we proceeded. He lit a four-foot candle and held it aloft as we walked. At one point I was horrified to find, grotesquely near my face, human skeletons—adults and children—embedded in hollows scooped in the tunnel's earthy wall. There were hundreds of them as we went deeper and deeper into the tunnel.

Returning to Bombay I set about my work immediately, picking up the thread of political events that had occurred while I was away. I called for old newspaper clippings from the reference section to find out who was fighting with whom, what were the new parties that had sprung up, and to learn new acronyms such as PPK, SSM, JPN and so on, which stood for names of parties. I needed to update myself about certain new policies and legal terms.

Actually, nothing new had happened. There were the usual speeches by ministers eternally promising drinking water, housing and also issuing warnings to anti-social elements. As usual, funds were missing or inadequate to finance the projects of the Five Year Plans. Delegations were going abroad looking for funds to cover our deficits. There were frequent riots and industrial unrest.

On the whole it seemed I had left my drawing board only a couple of days ago. I began to do my routine work as if there had been no break at all.

The nightmare of a political cartoonist is the deadline which haunts every newspaper office. He has to read the papers, analyse events, wait for his satirical idea to dawn, complete the cartoon and meet the deadline so that his efforts appear in the morning edition.

I had not only to show the ministers who mooted policies or programmes, I also had to convey the reactions of those who were affected by government programmes—namely the masses. Each time I had to show in my cartoon not one Indian citizen but several: Tamils, Gujaratis, Bengalis, Punjabis, Maharashtrians. All were

Indians of course but their looks, habits, dress varied vastly. I had to draw quite a crowd to indicate the common citizen. Sometimes when I had to work against time because I wasn't inspired early enough in the day, I used to reduce the number of these common citizens. Gradually the reader came to know that the crowd, however small, represented the people. I eliminated a few more in the course of time. Finally there was only one left. He was bald and bespectacled, his bulbous nose propped above a bristly moustache. He had a permanently bewildered look and was dressed in a dhoti and a checked coat. This man finally minimized my deadline agonies and took over the strenuous task of representing the mute millions of the country.

I had always toyed with the idea of creating a cartoon which would be broad-based and reach out to a large number who had hazy notions about political events at national and local levels.

The Common Man, who had been appearing for some years off and on in my political cartoons whenever his presence was necessary, had endeared himself to the readers of the *Times of India*. I thought he would be ideally suited for my purpose. In this new venture I was thinking of I would find scope to comment on a variety of issues, from scarcity of essential commodities and wasteful foreign jaunts by ministers to local civic problems of clearing the garbage and filling up the potholes on the roads. I planned it as a single column cartoon with the Common Man in various situations appearing everyday.

I mentioned my proposal to the editor, expecting some resistance. But to my amazement he was so carried away by the idea that he wanted to start it the very next morning.

I was alarmed. I had thought of this project only superficially in my fanciful moods. I knew that once I started it there would be no stopping. I had to keep going day after day for three hundred and sixty-five days. It would be a shameful professional defeat, a blot on my reputation if I gave it up halfway.

I asked the editor for more time. I decided the idea should be simple yet telling, and should not strain the readers' political understanding. I should bring down from their lofty heights, the national, international and local events and render them accessible to the common people. Here I would exercise my liberty to exaggerate freely, deviate from facts if that was going to help raise a laugh, indulge in fantasy to depict the ironies and paradoxes in the human situation.

I was all set to start the feature. We fixed a day for its first appearance, its position on the front page of the paper. On the spur of the moment I hit upon the title 'You Said It' for the cartoon. It received the unqualified approval of all concerned!

But the whole grand plan nearly got jolted out of existence when a letter arrived from London. It was from the editor of the *Evening Standard*, and it read: 'Dear Mr Laxman, I have been impressed by some of your cartoons in the *Times of India*. I would be interested to know if the idea of working in this country appeals to you. If so I would very much like you to consider joining us . . .'

It was a flattering offer, no doubt, being invited to take the place of David Low who had moved to the *Daily Mail*. My spirits soared, and all ideas for 'You Said It' vanished. My thoughts now were focused on plans to leave for London. All my colleagues looked at me as if I had been reincarnated as something of a superhuman being.

Gradually as the news spread, congratulatory messages started pouring in. One or two well-wishers even prophesied that it wouldn't be long before I emigrated to America—the ultimate destination of all young Indians.

As days passed, the novelty of my new role wore off. The thought of having to live in England began to bother me. People who were celebrating my potential British citizenship had no idea of the nature of my work. Perhaps they thought of me as one among the doctors, engineers, businessmen, shopkeepers who happily emigrated and continued to do their work abroad. But mine was a different profession. The conformity and uniformity of that country's social life and the propriety in political conduct would have reduced me to a mediocre illustrator of events. I would have missed the multifaceted, colourful life of India, whether social or political, that I lived with and understood. Finally I decided that it would be a great mistake to uproot myself and succumb to the glamour of living in a foreign country.

At the same time I dreaded the idea that one day in the future I might deeply regret that I had missed a golden opportunity by rejecting the *Evening Standard's* offer, succumbing to patriotic hallucinations.

I wrote to our London correspondent that I would soon be joining the *Evening Standard*. I asked for his advice regarding finding a decent apartment, information about the general working conditions in the *Standard* office, and for clarification of a million other doubts that harassed me night and day.

He was quick to reply, saying, 'It was very pleasant to hear from you, though the kind of queries you want me to answer are rather awkward. You already know something of the reputation of the *Evening Standard* for quick changes. You must, of course, keep this in mind before entertaining any offer from them, though I dare say your experience with them will be happier . . . Apart from uncertainty, in any Beaverbrook paper the working conditions are, I believe, very good . . .'

The letter did not help me much in taking a decision. The phrase 'the reputation of the *Standard* for quick changes' seemed to caution against taking the foolish step of joining a company known for sacking and arbitrary transfers. But it was cancelled by the sentence that followed, 'I dare say your experience with them will be happier . . . in any Beaverbrook paper the conditions of work, I believe, are very good . . .' which kindled the temptation to accept the offer.

I was once more caught in the same dilemma. I thought the best course would be to postpone the decision. I dashed off a letter to the editor of the *Standard*, stating that due to certain personal affairs which would take some time to sort out, I needed a little more time. I suitably wrapped up the letter in vagueness.

But people around me believed I was busy preparing for my departure. They threw farewell dinners and arranged cocktail parties. I went about joking and radiating cheer, without revealing my inner turmoil and confusion.

A couple of weeks later a cable from the *Evening Standard* brought relief providentially: 'Regret unable to continue negotiations stop circumstances have arisen which prevent our proceeding further with the proposal stop be assured it was not due to any reassessment of the value of your work stop.'

My problem was thus amicably settled through no effort of mine. I plunged into my routine life with renewed vigour.

My diligently-planned new single-column feature 'You Said It' started to appear. I worked with great gusto, freed from real characters like ministers and bureaucrats. I invented my own symbols for these. I liberated myself from the shackles of habitual realism, and indulged in a sort of political fantasy.

I began by tackling the local civic problems such as garbage clearing, water shortage, unattended drainage. Bombay roads were particularly known for their bad up-keep and notorious for potholes. But that seemed to be the state of roads all over the country. I did a cartoon on this subject many years ago which even today is talked about and reprinted in periodicals. It showed an astronomer peeping through a huge telescope at the pitted volcanic surface of the moon; the caption read, 'There must be some civic life on the moon. Look at all those potholes!'

For a long time I believed I was providing the readers with some comic relief in their dreary humdrum existence. The bespectacled Common Man in his checked coat had walked into my cartoon spontaneously, as if I had no hand in his creation. Equally effortlessly he became a silent spectator of events, moving with ease from drought-stricken villages to the airport to watch foreign delegations arriving, from the prime minister's banquet hall to peep at the visiting dignitary dining, to observing the suffering of the denizens of the slums. A few times he had even accompanied politicians when they went abroad. Once he even visited the South Pole along with a minister for commerce who held bilateral talks with a group of attentive penguins.

In the course of time I was surprised to discover that my readers looked upon me not merely as a cartoonist who tickled their sense of humour, but as a profound thinker, a social reformer, a political scientist, a critic of errant politicians and so on. I received letters complaining about postal delays, telephones, the sloppiness of municipal authorities, inflated electric bills, bribes in school admissions. One such letter pleaded, 'Please halt the 47 Down train at — for a few minutes to save me the bother of waiting four hours for the next one to go home from the office.'

Then there was an admirer of my cartoons who sent me three rupees by money order, apologizing that he was poor and could not afford more. This was a token gesture he made whenever he found a cartoon worthy of his appreciation.

I was greatly moved by the poor man's generosity, and I thought the best way to thank him would be to send him a set of *You Said It* volumes with my compliments. His reaction was quite unexpected. He briskly replied that he did not expect any return favours for his monetary appreciation. That was the last I heard from him. He was deeply offended for some mysterious reason.

And there was a devout Christian who wanted me to design the marble headstone for his wife's grave. She had been a great admirer of my cartoons, he said. It was an awkward situation and I found it difficult to wriggle out of this strange assignment. Finally, I was able to talk my way out of it politely, using all my diplomatic skills.

But soon I had to face another equally embarrassing situation. A recluse who lived in the Kanheri Caves paid me a surprise visit one morning. He said he had been a practising criminal lawyer before he devoted his life to meditation. Desiring the tranquillity of solitude, he retreated to the isolated caves in the hills. He was robed in saffron. His forehead was splattered with sacred ash and vermilion and he had made himself look fierce, with matted hair and a flowing beard. An iron trident with jangling bells completed his ensemble. He wanted me to do a caricature of his venerable master. From his mendicant's sack he took out a faded photo of another bearded prototype and held it before me. Of course, I had no intention of obliging him. In a long-winded way I explained the technical difficulties and the limitations of a faded photo for my purpose. He was convinced and immediately left, saying he had to walk back all the way to the caves before sunset as he had taken a vow never to use a vehicle.

Another offbeat incident revealed that my cartoons, besides provoking laughter, had a mystic appeal to a section of the public. In those days betting on numbers was quite a popular pastime, though illegal. Gamblers made or lost fortunes speculating on New York Cotton figures opening and closing at the stock market. These people somehow saw the possible lucky combination of numbers in my cartoons. It went roughly along these lines—suppose there were four people in the cartoon on a particular day, with three looking one way and one the other way, that somehow provided sufficient clues for the gamblers to speculate accordingly.

Again, suppose a minister's table displayed three telephone instruments and two of the minister's fingers were visible, well, it was yet another pointer to prosperity. Thus the number of lamp-posts, cars in a street scene, people in a bus queue were all indicators to where the treasure lay.

One morning a fat fellow who looked like a trader, clad in an immaculate white kurta and dhoti with a gold chain adorning his neck, was waiting for my arrival at the office. He took out a sheaf of high-denomination currency notes and offered it to me, asking in return for the favour of just one glimpse of the following morning's cartoon. This would help him to read the mysterious number hidden in it and thus gamble ahead of his rivals and make his fortune. It was not difficult to get rid of this customer. All I had to do was bring up imaginary legal objections to such a transaction, as specified in my contract as an employee of the *Times of India*. Before I could continue my narration to point out the illegality of betting, the chap had left the room and scooted away.

As my work became widely popular it attracted the attention of discriminating readers and the thinking public. I received letters and phone calls from lawyers, city fathers, college professors, management consultants, economists and so on.

Social organizations such as the Rotary and Lions Club, and innumerable other similar institutions perpetually searching for a speaker eyed me as an ideal stopgap. Programme secretaries suffered the nightmare prospect of running out of speakers to adorn the stage when the weekly meetings inexorably approached. There were numerous hints and suggestions that I would be invited to address one of their meetings. The impression that I was a voluble speaker was wrongly based on the eloquence of my satirist's comments in my cartoons.

What they did not know was that behind those bold and

daring thoughts and laughter-provoking cartoons was a man who dithered and shied away at the sight of the gathering of a dozen people in front of him. I had never in my student days gone up on a stage to participate in debates, dramas or elocution contests. I was essentially a backbencher.

So now, if someone approached me under the misconception that I was an orator and asked me to address this or that group, I would say that I would be out of town, that I had an appointment with the dentist, that I had to go to the airport to receive an old relative, and so on. But these stock excuses could not keep at bay the host of organizations starved of speakers for the week.

I knew this kind of dodging would not work for long. One day a president or secretary of a club would force me to go up on the platform and face the audience. I visualized myself collapsing there out of sheer nervousness, perspiring and begging for water, making a fool of myself in full view of hundreds of spectators.

One day a couple of youngsters dropped in to invite me to be the chief guest at an annual school function. They said they were from a night school somewhere in the suburbs. Before I could select a suitable excuse from my bag of lies, one of them said, 'You don't have to make any speech, sir. It's just that all the boys are eager to see you. You only have to distribute the awards for the best essays.'

I was tempted—I felt it would be a good beginning in facing an audience at least. I would arrive at some obscure school in the suburbs, distribute the prizes with patronizing handshakes, mumble encouraging words and get away. I accepted the invitation. They were overjoyed and thanked me. Then they said that evening's speaker was a matinee idol!

After they left I felt somewhat let down. The movie star was bound to overshadow me! I would be just a dummy on the decorated stage. But it was too late to withdraw my acceptance of the invitation without hurting the youngsters and damaging my reputation.

A week later one of the boys turned up to show me the programme—welcome address, prayer, garlanding the guests, annual report read by the principal, plan for the coming year, distribution of prizes, and speech by the famous actor.

I did not know what moved me at that moment! I heard myself say, 'I think it would not be in order if I did not say a few words thanking the organizers for inviting me, and saying some encouraging words to the boys.'

'Please, sir. We will be extremely grateful if you say a few words about your profession.'

So I began to draft my short speech to describe the work-style of a cartoonist. It was just a ten-minute speech. But I spent night and day writing it, adding jokes, serious advice, anecdotes, and moralizing.

I memorized the whole speech and rehearsed it standing in front of the dressing table mirror. I even taped my recital, listened to it and corrected my pronunciation and emphasis. The whole idea was to make my oration seem casual and spontaneous.

On the appointed day I dressed in a grey suit and red tie and waited for the car to pick me up and escort me to the venue.

The auditorium was large and filled to capacity. I estimated there were more than five hundred people in the audience, gaping at the cine star. Not all were students as I had guessed but also faculty members and outside invitees.

When the introductory formalities were over, the movie star was invited to make his speech. He rose to his full six feet, humbly pressing his palms in grateful thanks to the applauding crowd. The audience listened to him in rapt silence. He gave a quick biographical sketch of himself; how he rose from humble beginnings to fame and success. He appealed to the younger generation to work hard, achieve their goals and bring credit to their parents and to India. Thus he went on for half an hour giving advice, quoting from the life of eminent thinkers, and liberally projecting himself as an example of hard work, devotion and selfless commitment to the nation. He returned to his seat to the thunderous explosion of clapping.

Then came my turn, starting with the distribution of prizes to the winners of the essay competition—a certificate, a writing set, a photo frame and so on. That done, I sat down trembling with nervousness, waiting to be summoned to give my ten-minute speech entitled, 'A cartoonist's view of life'.

I had not seen a mike at such close quarters before! The sea of faces staring at me and the silence surcharged with expectation made my knees wobble. Resting my elbows on the podium for support, I began, 'Friends, I feel greatly honoured to be here this evening. You might wonder what is a cartoonist and what sort of life he leads. Most of you must have seen a carpenter at work, a tailor stitching clothes, a bricklayer building a wall, a watch repairer, a motor mechanic and so on. But few, I am sure, have breathed down the neck of a cartoonist to observe his creative process. It would be a cruel act. For he is in the throes of creation, waiting in agony. It would be like asking a man in the dentist's chair, "Do you mind, sir, if I watched your molars being extracted? . . ."'

My humour struck home! I waited for the din of clapping to subside, and continued. I was a different person, miraculously transformed. No longer a self-effacing, shy individual, I began to give a freewheeling talk, departing from the one I had got by heart. I stretched my speech for more than thirty minutes, punctuating it with wit and sprinkling it with anecdotes. I would have gone on and on but for a glance at the huge clock on the wall! Appreciation and applause were showered on me with bouquets and garlands. I romped home triumphant that evening.

It was my beginning as an orator. Within a year I had spoken at all the local clubs, association meetings, colleges and schools. Similar institutions all over the country extended invitations to address political scientists, economists, industrial magnates, management experts, sales representatives, travel agents. Perhaps bored with listening to speeches about their own professions, they found what I said refreshingly unconventional, unique and entertaining for a change. Later I began to give sketching demonstrations at the end of my speech, caricaturing political leaders, which became an added bonus for the organizers.

Later on I went to the US, the UK, Germany, Austria and Australia on a similar mission. One of my best moments was when I was invited by Heidelberg University. Late at night I was to be picked up from the airport and driven to the city about forty kilometres away. I didn't know who was coming to receive me. People were crowding the exits of the terminal. As I stood with my luggage wondering what to do,

I saw someone holding a huge placard showing my Common Man, in the semi-darkness of the receiving area. The person holding it was one of the university professors who was to drive me to Heidelberg. He thought that this was the easiest way to attract my attention and welcome me, he said.

*

The United States Information Service extended an invitation to visit America. I thought of the American cartoonists I would have the chance to meet. I was familiar with some of the well-known names, but I had always felt the quality of their work as political commentators lacked depth and satirical content. They were visually obvious, with a good number of dragons, vultures, fat figures and undefined beasts representing various forces that served the cartoonist to illustrate economic recession, political tussles, trade barriers, and Communism. Compared to their European and British counterparts, most American cartoons seemed rather naïve. But it was amazing that in the field of comic strips, animated films and social themes in the *New Yorker*, the Americans were far ahead as one saw.

One fine day I was flown to Kentucky in the south-central part of the country. I was to stay in Louisville and associate myself with one of the major newspapers in the town. No one explained exactly what my role in the newspaper office was to be. No one questioned me when I absented myself. I often went to loaf around Cherry Street, Chestnut Avenue, Blueberry Lane, as the streets were named. When I attended the office I just hung around chatting with a few friendly people, or wandered through the editorial department, reporters' desks or the printing press in the basement of the building.

I was not expected to draw cartoons for the paper. They had a political cartoonist on the staff. Some days I attended editorial conferences and paid undivided attention to the discussions, without understanding much since these dealt with local affairs. The cartoonist also participated in these sessions and took notes. When he went back to his room he sweated over three or four rough ideas and took them to the editor for approval. He returned to the room after the editor had chosen one of the ideas and suggested alterations and improvements. Then he worked on the approved piece till late in the evening. His style was laboured and archaic—full of dark shades like some eighteenth-century engraving.

I found Louisville a conservative town, not at all like the America of my impression gathered from movies and magazines. Everyone I met was friendly and warm and took me out to dinner and lunch, and even to the famous Kentucky Derby, the horse race, a national event.

I stayed on here for over a month. Before leaving I also gave an interview to the paper, illustrating my impressions with a few sketches. Of course, I depicted my Common Man in the streets of Louisville and visiting some local landmarks.

The press baron held a dinner just before I left. He invited the elite. He had a mansion surrounded by acres of gardens, with a private brook gushing through a cluster of weeping willow trees. He took me around the estate. The moon was up in the sky, and its silver reflection shimmered in the water. From the dark silhouette of the distant mansion came the murmur of guests at the cocktail hour. The hour had a magic spell and I stood there absorbing the charm of the moment. When the baron, who was showing me around the garden, said in a low musical voice, '. . . and out again I curve and flow to join the brimming river, for men may come and men may go, but I go on for ever . . .', I was taken aback! I could not have associated this hard-boiled corpulent American business tycoon with Tennyson and his poem 'The Brook'!

When we both returned to the drawing room to join the other guests they were high on bourbon whisky, singing and banging on the piano keys. While the jollity was in full swing, a luxurious limousine pulled up at the portico. A chauffeur opened the rear door and an old lady got out. The baron signalled to everyone to hide their drinks. By the time she ambled up the steps and came into the hall we were wiping our lips and standing about like good boys. The baron kissed her and conducted her to a seat. She greeted the people around her. Then the baron requested her with great deference to play something on the piano, which she gladly did. While I was wondering why the baron was making all this fuss about an old lady, the person next to me whispered, 'She is his mom.' She was visiting Louisville to attend the Southern Baptist convention that was going on. While she was thumping the piano keys and crooning a hymn, I saw the baron handing out teacups to everyone. When I got mine I found it contained bourbon. The baron whispered, 'Mummy is very religious and wouldn't like anyone drinking. Particularly when the convention is on . . .' and gave me a naughty wink.

For the first few days in New York I ventured out with fear gripping my heart. Having heard horror stories about crimes that took place in the city's alleys, each person I saw in the street seemed a goon, a gangster or a strangler. The ambience seemed favourable for such happenings. But after a few days the faces of the blacks, the whites, the bluish grey (effect of dope I presumed) seemed human and friendly. Even automobiles tearing past seemingly intent on killing unwary pedestrians came to a dead halt in a second as you crossed in front of them. Their smiling drivers would wave you on to safety to the opposite kerb. After some time I began to realize that the gruff exterior of New Yorkers had nothing to do with their basically compassionate soft inner self. Once during my wanderings I lost my way, and approached a chap leaning against a lamp-post reading a newspaper. I asked him for directions. He fixed me with his stare and barked unexpectedly, 'It's a big place. Where exactly do you want to go?' Surprised by his aggressiveness, I took a couple of steps backward. When I gave him the address he did not know where it was. He asked a passer-by. He too was ignorant. Then he took the trouble of taking me along to a drugstore where he made enquiries. He came out and gave me the exact route to my destination. I thanked him profusely. 'You are welcome. Now don't lose your way,' he said and went back to lean against his lamp-post again, assuming his grim exterior.

One day I was asked to dine with a famous theatre director. He was working on my brother Narayan's *The Guide*, to be staged on Broadway. He was rich and famous, and as befitting his status he lived on Park Avenue. I arrived at his place early in the evening, smartly dressed in a dark suit. The liveried doorman stopped me. I told him the name of the person I had come to visit, expecting this to soften his stiffness. But he called the two lift men in black bow ties and tailcoats standing at the end of the carpeted, flower-bedecked corridor. They came and looked me up and down and asked me to take the service lift at the back entrance. I protested and demanded an explanation. One of them asked, 'Aren't you Mexican?' Proudly, I identified my nationality. 'Oh, you are an Indian maharaja, are you? Hey, why don't you give me a job in your palace?' All of them laughed at my discomfiture. Insulted, humiliated, red in the face, I went back to my hotel. I phoned the director and apologized for not being present at the dinner. I told him about the outrageous behaviour of the chaps at the apartment entrance. He was shocked and apologized and insisted I should come back immediately. He assured me that everything would be all right.

I went back to Park Avenue. I found all three men standing sheepishly bowing and apologizing over and over. 'Sorry, sir, extremely sorry, sir. It was a misunderstanding, sir. No ill-feeling, sir . . .' they kept repeating, following me as I walked, poker faced, to the lift. I paid no attention and stepped into the lift regally. As it was going up, the operator said, 'The whole misunderstanding was because you were carrying a raincoat, sir. No one who comes through the front entrance carries anything. So you were mistaken for a service hand, sir. So sorry . . .'

Years later I happened to visit Boston to attend a seminar. There I accidentally met an Indian browsing in a bookshop. His ears perked up when I spoke in Kannada to a friend who was with me. The stranger approached me, introduced himself as a Mysorean, and asked if I was one too.

The brief contact landed me in New York as the house

guest of the Mysorean. Ironically, his apartment was in an apartment block in the same area of Park Avenue where I had the altercation with the doorman in another block of aprtments. Since those days Park Avenue had apparently become democratic, liberal and friendly towards brownskins carrying raincoats. I was told quite a few Asians had come to occupy these apartments since my last visit.

My host had been brought up and educated in the USA. His father was a pioneer immigrant and had been a citizen for over five decades. Now my friend was the vice president of a top American financial institution. His wife, cook, houseboy were all from Mysore. He narrated Kannada folk tales to his children and sang patriotic or religious songs in the evenings. Everyone spoke flawless Kannada in the house as if they were living in a Mysore village. My host spoke English without an American accent, surprisingly, considering he had lived there all his life.

As the evening approached I instinctively felt that this fellow was a teetotaller. So I asked him if I could have a couple of drinks before dinner. He said he had no objection, but there was no liquor in the house. I said I always carried a bottle for just such a contingency. He asked the children who were watching TV to go and play in their room when I sat down with the bottle. He said he had hardly been in his home town of Mysore, but had travelled to every nook and corner of the globe fixing, supervising and improving the financial fortunes of his company. He was held in very high esteem in his organization. I was amazed at how he had managed to live all his life in the US without being influenced in the least by the world outside Mysore.

I had come across quite a few similarly odd characters

in my travels. My view of the Empire State building, the Statue of Liberty, the Golden Gate Bridge or the Grand Canyon would be no different from that of a tourist, but having been habituated to oddities in human situations, I could not help focusing on the comic aspects of my fellow men and things around them. In a newspaper interview describing my impressions of Los Angeles seen from the window of a plane, for instance, I remarked, 'I saw the city in the deadly grip of a giant octopus with vast concrete tentacles, writhing and squeezing, from which panicky little autos were scuttling to safety.' The reporter exclaimed, 'Hey, is that your impression of our city? You are talking of the flyovers and criss-crossing highways seen from the air, aren't you? That's funny . . .' Then in the course of the interview I mentioned the contradictions I saw. I mentioned a wealthy industrialist friend in Chicago who showed me a couple of Picassos worth millions hanging in his drawing room. And yet he went about in an old battered Ford! As a contrast to this I saw a shimmering latest model of a Pontiac pull up in front of the Indian Embassy in Washington. A woman got out of it. It was the charwoman who had come to dust and clean up the Embassy.

An extension of similar opposites I saw in Berkeley, as I sat on a park bench near Ashbury Avenue, known as the home of the hippies.

An elderly hippie came and sat next to me. I stared at him unabashedly without fear of being misunderstood. Hippies wanted just that. Public attention sustained them. He was wearing an old turtleneck pullover, rows and rows of coloured beads, medallions, emblems, stickers with slogans crying out for a better world. The upper part of his face was covered by a cascade of unkempt hair, the middle with dark goggles and the lower part with a luxuriant dark beard. Through all these he managed to reveal a friendly smile. In the course of our conversation I gathered that he hated affluence. He had done away with furniture and other luxury items in his apartment. He sent his children to an overcrowded neighbourhood school in a poor quarter of the city. His family ate breakfast, lunch and dinner off the cooking range, dispensing thus with dining table and chairs. His car was a five-year-old second-hand Chevrolet. 'You see how free I am. A poor man is a free man, he has no obligations and no responsibility.' I was dumbfounded listening to him and the remotely Gandhian philosophy he had arrived at on his own.

It was when I met another friend who had once been a consular officer in Bombay, that I realized how hard it was to remain in a state of poverty in that country, with all the golden opportunities there were to get rich. My friend drove me to his suburban home. On the way he told me he had done very well since retirement and was now the head of a flourishing industry. He had a large house, a vast garden full of trees and flower beds. His fifteen-year-old son was mowing the lawn and piling up the cut grass neatly in a corner.

When we had settled down in the living room and were recalling the time he had spent in India, the young fellow arrived with a tray carrying drinks. He passed around snacks and cigarettes and took care of us with great care and courtesy. When he was not attending to us he lounged on a distant sofa and kept an alert eye on us, jumping up to serve our needs. At the dining table he hovered round us, and when we returned to the sitting room after dinner he brought coffee and liqueur. Making sure we needed nothing else that evening, he took our leave most courteously and went in to help his mother clear the table.

I was astonished at the boy's sense of duty and helpful nature. I complimented the parents for instilling such a helpful attitude in their son.

My friend laughed and said, 'Sure, Jim is helpful. He gets paid to do all this around the house. He is a smart guy. He makes such a lot helping us, he invests it all in stocks! If I don't watch out he will buy up my company one day!'

On one of my visits to the US I thought it wouldn't be a bad idea to go to Canada to see the great Niagara Falls. I was told it was as easy as calling on a friend across the street. All I had to do was fly to Buffalo, check into a hotel, walk across the border into Canada. It was that easy, I was given to understand.

I had seen the Grand Canyon, magnificent Mount Everest on a clear day, the Alps and so on. Those were unforgettable experiences. Niagara almost remained an unfulfilled wish, thanks to a petty immigration clerk in the Canadian Embassy in New York! But it was made more memorable than I bargained for! After an endless wait to obtain the necessary forms for a visa, and hours of standing in a queue made up of Japanese, Indians, Mexicans, Africans, Chinese and people of other races, my turn finally came. I was shown into a narrow cubicle where a thin anaemic fellow, with long brown hair and blue eyes, was sitting with my passport and papers. When he had examined the documents, he suddenly asked, 'So you want to go to Canada?'

'Yes,' I said.

'Why? I wish to know why you want to go to Canada.'

'To see the Niagara, of course,' I said.

He continued the interrogation. 'Just to see the Niagara. I see. Then why did you not get the visa in your own country if you were so keen on seeing it?'

I explained that there was no Canadian consulate in Bombay (at that time there wasn't).

'That we all know. Then why didn't you go to Delhi to get it from our Embassy there?' He seemed determined to get to my secret mission to Canada. He triumphantly fixed me with his cold gaze and waited for an answer. I could see he was enjoying the role of an inquisitor, borrowing the style from such types in war movies.

'I did not decide to visit Niagara till a few days ago . . .'

'But you made such a major decision to step into Canada just like that, after coming to New York? Strange! Very strange! . . . You have any friends in Canada?' I replied in the negative. He probed further. 'Any relatives?' I said 'No!' curtly. He said, 'Are you sure?' I was getting tired of his inane, endless questions and replied, 'Wouldn't I know if there was a relative of mine in any part of the world?'

'Maybe. But I am interested in your relatives in Canada!' he snapped, surpassing himself in illogic. Then he asked for my identity card. I told him there was no such thing in our country. The passport that he held should serve the purpose. 'Then please show me a letter from your employers.' Naturally I couldn't produce such a letter either. By now I had decided to abandon my plans to see the Falls, so I sat back to relish his stupidity. 'May I have the address of your hotel, please.' I gave it to him and asked him to phone and find out if I was telling the truth. 'Oh no, we have no time for all that.' Then he asked how long I proposed to stay in the US. When exactly was I going back to India? Had I booked my return passage? If not, why not? How much money was I carrying? I gave varied answers-irresponsible, funny, sarcastic, tongue-in-cheek, mock-serious. But my wit was lost on this bureaucrat. He took my frivolous replies seriously, without surprise or a smile. When I thought I had had enough of this fellow, I got up and snatched my passport and documents from his hands, saying, 'Keep your Niagara to yourself. I don't want to see it.' I was about to walk out when he said, 'No offence meant. These are routine questions. I am only doing my duty.' He held out his hand for my papers and duly stamped them for my entry into Canada!

India's political scene has always provided ample grist for the satirical cartoonist's mill.

The leaders of our nation put their heads together and drew up a Constitution and declared India a sovereign, united, secular democratic republic. But they soon set about fragmenting the nation on a linguistic basis. Then they got busy changing the age old names of the streets, highways, public buildings, parks. The idea was to wipe out the historical fact of our having once been the colonial subjects of the British. All the names were changed to the names of those who fought for our freedom. Then they wanted all India to forget English and talk in Hindi, which was declared the national language.

All these and many more perverted priorities kept the common man in suspense, confusion and untold misery. But their policies kept the cartoonist busy. While the nation was facing such uncertainties, politically, economically and socially, the Chinese intruded into our territory. Pakistan attempted to nibble away at Kashmir, and the Portuguese in their colony of Goa tried to dig in their heels and stay on in the face of hopeless odds. All these offered a rich fare to the cartoonist whose comments were eagerly looked forward to by the readers of the paper.

As if there was not enough trouble the colossus, the Indian National Congress, showed signs of cracking up. Infighting, betrayals and factionalism were the order of the day. Even a seasoned leader like Nehru threatened to resign from the leadership of the nation and the party, out of sheer disgust with his followers. My pictorial comments on these happenings over the years were overflowing from the cupboard where I kept them in grand disorder. Suddenly it occurred to me that it would be a good idea to select some for a book of cartoons, which would depict a satirical history of a period of our nation's history.

With this intention I spread the cartoons out and prepared to select the best ones. Then I realized the extent of my carelessness—I had been just shoving the cartoons in the cupboard as they came each day after publication, without indexing or putting a date on them. I despaired as to how to bring some order into this chaos. However, the accidental positioning of some cartoons as they lay on the table amused me. A cartoon of the Berlin blockade had fallen next to one showing Vinoba Bhave fasting in protest against cow slaughter. There were many other such absurd juxtapositions.

Besides failing to arrange my cartoons in an order, I could not decide which was my best effort and which was poor. What struck me as brilliant a moment ago and made me indulge in self-congratulation on my creative genius appeared embarrassingly poor on a second look.

Wading through the sea of dog-eared sketches, I had to face another problem. Some of the cartoons made no sense at all. What in heaven's name could they be referring to? Perhaps it had brought national applause on the day it was flashed on the front page of the *Times of India* under the mast-head. Perhaps the political clown shown in one cartoon was a chief minister of a minor state or a junior in the Central cabinet, whose indiscretion and irresponsible pronouncements might have invited the attention of the whole nation including that of mine, inspiring me to do the cartoon. This character must have since disappeared from the political scene; no trace of him existed now except the frayed drawing I held puzzling over!

I was also nagged by the proliferation of acronyms. I had inscribed Cong (SDK), LB, KPSS, ABWU, OPPUWF and so on, across the shirts of the leaders, their coat sleeves, on tattered flags, on tigers, pythons, bulls. The letters stood for a new party that had been floated, or splinter groups from the main party. Of course, by the time I came to learn what the acronyms represented, the entities they signified had already vanished from the national political scene.

It is the nature of political cartoons to have a very short life, except those few, of course, which satirize momentous national events such as the Partition, India's linguistic divides, the dissolution of princely states, the Emergency.

Unable to edit my own book of cartoons, I left the project to more competent hands and settled down to studying current events and churning out my daily contributions.

The tension that was building up between India and Pakistan on the western border exploded into a war. Guns boomed and bombs were dropped. The superpowers tried to cash in on the crisis through intrigues and threats, tilting their support to one side and warning the other. The war finally ended after twenty-two days. A few weeks later, along with some of my colleagues, I went on a tour of war-ravaged border areas. Our army still held on to some Pakistani territory. Soldiers stood facing their Pakistani counterparts within shouting distance!

I saw a shattered bunker. The gun inside had been blown up, and the concrete walls were splashed with blood.

Some Indian soldiers were cooking their midday meal nearby, while a pack of stray dogs were hovering around, waiting for a chance to get at leftovers. In that grim ambience, I was tickled to see a few of these mongrels boldly trot through the barbed wire fence into Pakistan, to taste the crumbs tossed by those soldiers having their meal.

Later the Army PRO accompanied us to a badly damaged house with pock-marked walls. It belonged to a Pakistani lawyer who had been evacuated at the time of the war. We sat in his roofless drawing room to have our tea and sandwiches. I inspected the family photographs still hanging on the walls. There was one of an anonymous lawyer, a young man in an academic gown—presumably taken on the occasion of his getting the law degree.

Then we moved on to the other section of border towns, Fazilka, Sulemankia, Amritsar. We entered Lahore from the Wagah check post. The buildings on either side of the main street were damaged. Twisted bicycles, handcarts, blown-up cars and buses lay on the road. Heaps of shoes, sandals and broken crockery were strewn all over the place.

We wandered around till late evening. Our PRO cautioned me that I would be a sitting duck for a sniper, in my white bush shirt against the dark background. So we hurried back. But I lagged behind a bit, collecting spent bullets and brass shell cases lying around.

The next day we returned to Delhi. On the way we stopped at Khemkaran to see a whole field of battered and disembowelled Sherman tanks, dotted all over the place like dead beetles. During this brief visit I made several sketches of dilapidated bridges, buildings, bunkers, tanks, soldiers on guard. Some of these appeared later in the *Illustrated Weekly*, and a full page was devoted to these war sketches in the *Times of India*.

When Mrs Gandhi took over as the prime minister, I found her frail, laconic and withdrawn. I wondered if she would ever be able to assert her power and prove a match for senior congressmen who were supporting her for their own selfish ends. Regardless of her political role, I found her personality extremely amenable to caricature.

Much to everyone's surprise, she quickly consolidated her strength and upset the devious calculations of the old congress stalwarts. By having the President of India of her choice and causing a staggering jolt to the cabinet by unceremoniously sacking some who believed they were unassailable, she proved to be the supreme leader of the Congress party and the nation. She continued the momentum of her success by nationalizing the banks, withdrawing privy purses and, above all, defeating Pakistan in East Bengal and creating Bangladesh.

I greatly enjoyed her style of functioning. I ridiculed and poked fun at every move she made, for that was my business as a cartoonist. She gave me ample opportunity to wield my brush unsparingly. In course of time word trickled in that she felt I was rather unkind to her in my comments. I could not help it, as it is not the job of any cartoonist worth his salt to glorify any political head of state in a democracy. The art of political satire was based on disapproval and complaint. And so I continued to attack the establishment.

A few months later a man rang my doorbell at home and introduced himself as an official from the home ministry, New Delhi. He said he had brought the good news that the PM had approved the list of Padma Bhushan awardees, and my name was included in it. I was stunned; here I was attacking and making fun of her in my cartoons, and she had seen fit to confer this honour on me!

I suspected a catch in this somewhere! The official saw my hesitation and sensed my misgivings. He said he wanted my formal acceptance so he could make the official announcement. I asked for a little more time to decide. I feared that I was being bought by the establishment. I would be obliged to Mrs Gandhi and have to show restraint in my free comments if I accepted the honour. My senior colleagues in the office felt the same way and urged me to decline it. But my elders at home were overjoyed and advised me to accept the title, saying that my brother Narayan was already a Padma Bhushan and that my mother would be proud to have two of her sons awarded national recognition.

Finally I agreed to accept the honour. The official announcement was made and congratulatory messages poured in from all parts of the country.

Soon a circular from the home minister followed from Delhi, asking me to be present in the capital for rehearsals for the investiture ceremony; I would be paid first class non-a/c fare to and fro. I was entitled to a stipend of eleven and a half rupees if I arrived at Delhi in the forenoon of the day, and twenty-two rupees if I happened to be there earlier. And if I was to bring my spouse I had to bear the expenses of her travel, and on the day of the function she should dress soberly, wearing a saree whose border should not to be more than two inches broad!

Fortunately I was spared the ordeal of attending the rehearsal as well as the investiture ceremony, as I had accepted an invitation to visit Germany at that time.

Ten months later the citation declaring I was a Padma Bhushan, and two medals—one big and another small—were delivered by a postman to my flat. There was a note from the home secretary stating that the big medal was to be worn for formal functions and the small one on informal occasions. However, it hinted that neither should be displayed conspicuously. I am still to understand what these instructions meant!

The years that followed were normal as far as my functioning as a cartoonist was concerned. There was no interference from Delhi as I feared. I continued with my critical assessment of government functioning and policies. Mrs Gandhi started to lose her popularity and her grip over the country. Corruption, administrative blunders, inflation, the erosion of democratic values, riots, protests, strikes were rampant all over the country. India became a virtual paradise for the satirical commentator.

At this moment of crisis in Indira Gandhi's political career, the Allahabad High Court judgment set aside her election to the Lok Sabha. In despair she clamped the Emergency upon the nation, suspended the democratic Constitution, imposed censorship on the media, and imprisoned those who dared to oppose her.

Journalists, politicians and those whose loyalty was suspect found themselves behind bars.

The day the Emergency was declared, no one was able to clearly assess its implications, and how the state would function. Editors, writers and reporters were still guessing and debating its effect when I left for Bangalore to address a Rotary Club meeting that evening. A packed auditorium of Rotarians was waiting for me, expecting a hilarious speech caricaturing Mrs Gandhi's style of governing the country. They did not know the enormity of the situation we were in. I had prepared a most scathing attack on Mrs Gandhi and her cabinet ministers, interwoven with choice jokes and side-splitting anecdotes. But the president of the Rotary Club took me aside and cautioned me in whispers, urging restraint in my speech, advising me to avoid referring to the government. Then I noticed policemen standing at the doors and plainsclothes men among the audience.

Much to the disappointment and surprise of the audience, I gave an hour-long factual account of my visit to the Andaman and Nicobar Islands.

*

Providentially, my wife and I had visited those islands just a year or two earlier. The memory of our travels was still fresh, and I was able to hold forth effortlessly at the Rotary Club. If this subject had not occurred to me on the spur of the moment, and I had blundered on innocently with my original theme, 'The cartoonist's view of politics', I would perhaps have landed in jail. I would have certainly made some uncomplimentary and humorous remarks about the government, given a verbal caricature of Mrs Gandhi, described the cabinet as a bunch of buffoons, criticized the economy, red-tape, waste, corruption, etc. etc. All these issues affected the common citizen of India, and were ones with which I had been dealing for over three decades. Ironically, the penal settlement in the Andamans during the British raj provided ample subject matter for my talk at the Rotary meeting, and saved me from being arrested and imprisoned, cooling my heels without trial!

One day my wife was leafing through an atlas and suddenly she said, 'Let us take a trip to Andaman and Nicobar Islands.' I told my Rotarian audience that until that moment I did not even know those far-flung islands belonged to India! I thought it wouldn't be a bad idea to take an adventurous vacation in an out of the way place where no tourist normally went.

I did not know what to do next, or even whom to ask about the mode of travel, because there was no normal air or boat service to the islands. Even the Government of India's department of tourism had no clue to it. After many days of going about and enquiring, I finally found a person who gave us the barest of information. Clinging to it and working our way some days later we finally boarded a cargo ship at Madras leaving for Port Blair.

The Bay of Bengal was dark blue like carbon paper, speckled with tiny waves as far as the horizon. Seagulls and migratory birds busily criss-crossed the sky above the ocean. Occasionally I saw a school of flying fish darting like rockets over the ocean surface.

We sailed for five days. As we neared Chatham, dolphins danced around the hull of the ship and escorted us. Here and there one saw the menacing dark fins of sharks.

Thus I went on regaling the Rotarians with the story of my trip to the Andamans. I was pleased that they were listening with rapt attention, perhaps because the subject was for a change different from the usual tale of government blunders, red-tape, licences and permits etc.

I told them that in the Andamans we stayed in a makeshift dwelling belonging to a timber exporting company. We hired a boat to cover the length and breadth of the island: from the northernmost part called Rangath down to middle Andaman, Nicobar, Car Nicobar, and innumerable little islands, Kachal, Non Cowry, Komata, Carbinscove. All were surrounded by deserted beaches and shallow emerald-green lagoons. One could see sharks as clearly as if one was looking through the glass panes of a large aquarium. We explored the thick impenetrable jungle of the island's interior. The trees were gigantic both in height and girth and seemed to belong to the world of geology rather than botany. The jungles were free of snakes, tigers, lions and other wild animals. But there were Jarvas, the dreaded tribals. They were pathologically hostile and killed with bows and arrows any intruder encroaching on their territory in the western part of the Andamans.

On one of the islands I was surprised to find a Japanese bomber that had been shot down, presumably during World War II. The aircraft was thickly veiled with creepers and wild plants. When I went close to it I was startled by grunting noises and strange animals jumping out of the cockpit. They turned out to be wild pigs!

In another desolate jungle clearing I saw a graveyard. The roots of the vegitation had uprooted the headstone and shoved the marble grave aside, exposing a skeleton. The inscription on the headstone read, '*John Wood . . . Officer, East India Company, died 1817, age 25*'. The next one was of someone who had died in the year 1858, age twenty-seven. There was also the grave of a captain killed by a shark near Port Blair at the age of thirty-five. Of course, we visited the infamous Cellular Jail, saw the gibbet for hanging prisoners and Centennial Island where giant crabs climbed up the coconut trees, plucked the nuts, climbed down, husked them with their claws, cracked them and noisily ate the kernels!

I told the Rotarians I could have gone on describing that tropical paradise, but I had already spoken for more than an hour. I concluded my speech to thundering applause.

All the while I was worried about the Emergency, and was anxious to find out how the *Times of India* was functioning.

*

On returning to Bombay, I saw my desk copies of messages sent by the censor office in Delhi to the news editor in Bombay. The first one said, 'All stories, comments, editorials etc. on inter-party affairs in the Congress to be censored . . .' The second one declared, '. . . stories on insurgency in the north-east region not to be published . . .' And the third one read, 'Nothing should be published about the collapse of the TV tower in Raipur'.

Nearly all news about national activities was banned, with so many restrictions imposed I had to choose a subject far away from the shores of our land. I drew a cartoon about British politics and ridiculed Harold Wilson and the Labour Party. The censors passed it. Next day I did one on the population explosion. Thus I went on skirting vital issues so that I could escape the censors' rubber stamp.

I resigned myself to suspending all my critical judgement, my eye for absurdity and the healthy irreverence with which I was born. I began to offer the reader dull, puerile, senseless, silly ideas without content of humour or satire.

Despite my care and humbling myself abjectly before the censors, Delhi found some of my cartoons violating the rules. Immediately my name was removed from the state censorship list and put on the list supervised by the Central censor board.

After this change, even the simplest sketch showing a fat fellow slipping on a banana peel was not passed! Some timid, illiterate clerk played safe and banned my cartoons, fearing they might contain hidden meanings which might have proved beyond his intelligence, or he gave his own interpretation to them and censored them himself.

I decided to play safe. I did a cartoon flattering the government. I showed how, thanks to the Central civil supplies department and the ceaseless efforts of committed officials, the prices of essential commodities were tumbling down, much to the delight of the common man! This cartoon appeared in all editions of the paper. But soon I was running out of nice things to say about our rulers. I settled for some rather tame ones. I drew a fashionable lady wearing high heels which were so high that people had to bend backwards to see her face—very funny! Thus the quality of my cartoons went steadily from bad to worse.

Then suddenly the censors woke up and found me behaving in a very naughty manner when they were looking the other way! The cartoon on Harold Wilson was a cunning cover-up and was an implied, devious comment on Mrs Gandhi, they said. The one that paid tribute to the Central civil supplies department for bringing down prices was according to them a viciously tongue-in-cheek criticism of the government for not bringing down the soaring prices. And the cartoon in which a lady was shown in high heels was regarded as a blatant attempt to mock Mrs Gandhi. I was warned that if I continued to indulge in this sort of disruptive activity through my cartoons, I would regret it.

After such a senseless threat I shuddered to approach my drawing board. I was desperate for help and guidance, but I could not think of anyone safe to turn to. Finally I decided to approach Mrs Gandhi herself, to tell her I was no good at doing anything else, and that cartooning was my bread and butter.

Just as I was preparing the leave for Delhi, a letter arrived from the officials of the Central civil supplies department congratulating me on the cartoon that depicted the fall in prices, and requesting me to gift them the original so they could hang it proudly in their Central office. I was aghast! The situation could not have been more ridiculous. This was the cartoon over which the censors had breathed fire and brimstone and threatened to put me behind bars!

However, I met Mrs Gandhi and told her about my plight as a cartoonist, and submitted a memorandum listing the injustices committed by the censors. She was surprisingly kind and understanding. After blaming zealous bureaucrats, she said, 'You carry on with your work. In a democracy satirical comments are essential as checks and balances . . .'

I dashed out of the South Block with renewed zest to carry on my work as vigorously as before!

Arrests and imprisonments continued unabated. Editors who had wielded their pen courageously before the Emergency now quietly sat back in their chairs, not doing a stroke of work. So I decided it would be a wise decision to make use of the 'special freedom' bestowed on me by Mrs

Gandhi with great care and caution, and not put my luck to test.

Before returning to Bombay after seeing the prime minister I paid a visit to the Central Censor Office out of curiosity. It was in a vast hall in the secretariat building. There were numerous wooden cubicles, with only a pigeon-hole screening the person sitting inside. Those who came to get their articles, photographs, editorials, charts, speeches approved, handed them over to the censors through the pigeon-hole, receiving a numbered token in return. People waited anxiously in the corridor. Suddenly a voice would announce from one of the pigeon-holes, 'Twenty-eight, ninety-three, forty-seven . . .' and so on. People with these numbers would rush to the cubicles and exchange the token for their materials, and rip open the brown cover to see nervously if the items had been stamped 'censored' or not.

Returning to Bombay after receiving Mrs Gandhi's assurance, I began to take cautious risks. The censors passed my cartoons. Encouraged, I began to display some more boldness. Slowly my fears of the censor board receded, and I went back to my normal style of working, poking fun at our leaders, debunking their pronouncements and puncturing the ego which had been puffed up by the power they enjoyed under the Emergency.

Just then DK Barooah, the Congress president, gave me an excellent opportunity to ridicule him and demolish his observation. Delivering his speech at the seventy-fifth plenary session of the Congress at Chandigarh, he said something to this effect . . . 'India is Indira and Indira is India. The Emergency has banished from the nation the evil forces that were haunting it. The Emergency should be continued so that these ugly forces do not raise their heads again.' My cartoon on his deplorable speech appeared on the front page of the *Times of India* and a whole bundle of it landed at the venue of the plenary session.

Soon I received a phone call from the chief censor officer in Delhi. He said the delegates were greatly offended by the cartoon. They questioned the efficiency of the minister for information and broadcasting and his department in keeping vigil over the disruptive forces in the land.

Then the minister for information and broadcasting himself came to Bombay, and I was summoned to appear before him. I was told he would be at Raj Bhavan. But actually he was occupying a suite in a five-star hotel in the heart of the city. When I entered the luxurious room he did not even offer me a seat. He warned that if I got up to such mischief of poking fun at revered and respected Congress leaders, I would be thrown into prison. I mumbled that Mrs Gandhi had assured me . . . He brushed my feeble protest aside and thundered, 'I know all that. You are not above law. I have a job to carry out and I will do it, come what may.'

At that very moment I decided to retire from the business of cartooning. After all, I told myself, I had had a good innings in this field over the years, and had gained popularity both at home and abroad. I had been conferred with titles and awards. In my capacity as a cartoonist I had taken the opportunity to travel extensively in my own country as well as outside. So now I could, and perhaps should, retire without regrets. I had come to believe that the art of cartooning in India would in any case slowly become defunct under Mrs Gandhi's dispensation.

*

My wife was overjoyed when I announced I had decided to retire, taking all the leave available to me. She suggested going away from it all to Mauritius for a long, well-earned holiday.

I was preoccupied with a mixed feeling of relief that I would no longer be subject to the censors' indignities and torments, and at the same time with a deep remorse that my diligently built career over the years had to end so ingloriously! However, we left for Mauritius, some 4500 kilometres south-west of Bombay. The prospect of a long journey began to seem very tedious. My mind began to revolve around plans for the future. I resolved to devote all my time to painting, sketching, writing novels. I told myself that I had wasted three decades ignoring these creative fields and done the thankless job of opposing our country's politicians.

Largely politics was the profession of school drop-outs; I observed that politicians were endowed with immense vitality but little intelligence. Stretching out in the aircraft's comfortable seat, I speculated that politicians were the most durable among the human species. They were tough, impervious to humiliation, failure, defeat, insults, shocks. They led a conscience-free existence hungering eternally for power even when charged with corruption, fraud and murder! For all the travelling they did all over the subcontinent, eating and sleeping at odd hours and shouting themselves hoarse in front of a battery of microphones in heat and dust and sub-zero temperatures, they never suffered from colds, sore throats, fevers or any such maladies that afflicted the common citizen. Thus I mused critically, judging, making uncharitable, abusive mental notes about the very people who just by being themselves, had generously provided me with bread and butter and brought me rewards and fame. I did not have to study their faces anymore or read their pretentious speeches.

But at the same time I wondered that if by chance a brilliant satirical idea flashed across my mind, would it not be an agony to turn away from it because I had abandoned the art of cartooning?

I was thinking thus casually viewing the clouds outside the window as the aircraft skimmed over them. My age-old habit of looking at objects and visualizing their likeness to human shapes and faces gradually asserted itself. I began to see in the clouds—the heroes of the ancient legends of China, Rome, Greece, India. I saw the rippling muscles of Atlas bearing the globe on his mighty shoulders, and Hercules with his boundless vitality fighting a lion. And there was an enormous hooded cobra sheltering Vishnu. But it was rapidly melting, taking the form of a Chinese dragon. Among the leaping deer, elephants, horses and sheep there was Ganapati with his large head, flapping ears and fat and chubby torso, including the mouse at his feet.

Gradually the hum of the aëroplane changed, indicating it was about to land. I woke up from creating cloud sculptures. Soon we arrived at Mauritius.

Here I came across the most unique cocktail of human types and creeds—Africans, Arabs, Chinese, Germans, Dutch, French, English and, of course, Indians, all rubbed shoulders with one another without causing any friction, enjoying a peculiar sense of oneness. I met a chap whose name was Radha Krishna Govindan. I spoke to him in Tamil. He looked bewildered, and answered me in mangled English with a heavy French accent, perhaps mixed with Arabic and Dutch. Centuries ago his ancestors, like those of other Mauritians, had been shipped here as slaves or indentured labour. Mr Govindan of this century had no clue to the existence of Madras or the sounds of Tamil.

I liked Mauritius. It was a compact sixty kilometres wide and about fifty kilometres long. The roads were neat and straight, cutting through acres of sugarcane fields. An hour's drive in any direction brought you to the limits of the island. It was ringed by a coral reef in shallow blue water. It was a paradise for tourists from all over the world.

We went up a mountain to peep down a vast crater of a volcano that had long been safely dead sometime back in the geological past. It had left behind the most fascinating rock formations. Even the hills were freakish, not the common pyramidical shapes. These had knife-edge shapes sweeping upwards suddenly, then running flat and dropping vertically. Sometimes one saw a pin-point of a peak with hardly any support-base precariously balancing a boulder larger than itself, giving the feeling that it would topple over any minute and roll down to the township below!

Port Lewis reminded me of the great authors Joseph Gonrad and Somerset Maugham. This tiny port town seemed to be built at their suggestion to suit their novels and short stories.

Grimy seamen and dock hands ambled about the harbour or lounged against stacked oil drums and packing cases. It was an ideal place for me to sketch. Ropes hung like cobwebs from the masts of docked ships and trawlers. In the middle of the harbour loomed the statue of the founder of Mauritius—Maha de la Bombdonis in wig, frock coat and breeches.

Of all my Mauritian experiences, the most thrilling was a cruise in a glass-bottomed boat to explore the submerged coral reefs and marine life. To start with, quantities of seashells of all sizes were strewn on the yellow sand. Crabs scurried for shelter as we passed over them. Shreds of seaweed floated by. Then came the skeleton-like formations of coral. The sea deepened, becoming dark. Lobsters slithered below us. As the boat moved further into the sea, the scene turned eerie. The coral jungle became dense. I saw shapeless ugly creatures crawling in the dark depths of the sea bed. I felt their eyes watching me from behind giant marine bushes. There were headless creatures leading a plant life rooted to the ground, swaying from side to side in a ghastly manner. All of a sudden, a cheerful school of yellow fish with black stripes passed flicking their tails.

There were fields of coral, their branches tipped with blue, luminous as candles. Pink, yellow, purple fish lit up the water. But there were some with hideous spikes all over their bodies and some with faces as if they were smashed and battered. All of them had the look of condemned souls of sinners suffering eternal damnation in the weird twilight world of a nightmarish landscape.

Soon I could see through the glass familiar objects—shells, algae, cigarette packets, beer bottles . . . I got off the boat thanking my stars that I was not born a fish!

I had no newspapers, no radio. I spent all my time sketching the scenery around me, observing the locals and tourists and enjoying myself. Then I heard the news that the Emergency had been relaxed all over India, and there would soon be general elections.

As my wife and I boarded the plane for our return journey to Bombay, I was in a deep depression. I had hoped that Mrs Gandhi would continue forever as a dictator, giving me the excuse to enjoy my retirement. But now I was already feeling the compulsion to get back to work!

However, she lost the elections and the Janata Party came to power. I changed my decision and went back to my drawing board. The years that followed were most hilarious from a cartoonist's perspective!

*

The Janata Party took over the task of running the nation. Morarji Desai became the prime minister. The government was a conglomeration of a variety of groups with independent ideas; it failed to achieve a coherent, single identity.

The prime minister was outwardly supported by veteran leaders, but each one nurtured ambitions of pushing him out and occupying the seat of power. There were also smaller fry who made no secret of their disloyalty.

The Congress, now in the opposition, carried on with its usual business of infighting, betrayals, defecting, splitting and floating innumerable splinter factions as new offshoots of the Congress. As a result the rulers and the stalwarts in the opposition had to constantly watch over their shoulders for a possible stab in the back. They had no time to look in front at the country, and at the common man's needs. In the various

various states the situation was no different—so much so, that I had no problem getting a daily idea for my cartoon. The leaders at the centre as well as in the states were falling over each other, as it were, to help me out at my drawing board.

I was left with plenty of time to devote to my other activities, such as drawing crows, for which I have always had a fascination, painting various forms of the elephant god Ganapati, moulding his image in wax and plaster, writing short stories and travelogues. I also illustrated my brother Narayan's short stories and novels, and the children's stories written by my wife Kamala.

But my whole life changed one day because a cat fell into the reservoir situated at the top of the *Times of India* building. The cat rotted and polluted the water. Soon the office canteen which prepared tea, coffee, lunch and dinner for the employees of the *Times of India* was serving contaminated food. Consequently, four hundred and seventy cases of jaundice were reported within a fortnight. I was one of them!

Just before the calamity occurred, I had been busy looking for a suitable bride for my son Tikari. I was hoping that like most boys of his age, he would date a girl, get engaged to her, and marry. We had given him full liberty to choose whoever he fancied no matter what religion or belief. But the young man threw the ball in our court and asked us to look for a girl for him.

We began to consider feelers and hints from parents who had daughters of marriageable age. We personally saw a few of these girls. Most of them were good-natured, educated and sensible. But however hard we tried, the image simply could not form of the girl being Tikari's wife!

A couple of times the match was rejected by mutual consent. One girl was physically too large and my son was of normal height and weight. Another one was in a hurry to get married and immediately demanded a car of her own, an airconditioner in the bedroom, and many other items which are usually acquired over a lifetime. Yet another one was suffering from wounded emotion because her parents had frustrated her love affair with a boy. The parents were anxious to marry her off before she launched into another matrimonial adventure. This girl was pretty, but obviously moody. She scowled at her father, glared at her mother and snapped at us when we tried to converse with her.

One of our relatives suggested that to save all the bother the best thing would be to put an advertisement in the *Hindu*. He undertook to draft the advertisement, insert it in the paper and also receive the replies. He would select from them and submit to us what he thought was suitable.

I was still convalescing in bed a month after the attack of jaundice when his selection of seven arrived. After thoroughly scrutinizing and judging the alliances from all angles, my wife and I eliminated five. We examined the remaining two further, and finally chose one. And this girl became our daughter-in-law. Luckily our choice was perfect—all of us have lived ever since like friends in our joint family.

Meanwhile my job was becoming more and more difficult—not for want of ideas, but because there were too many of them. The concept of a minister had changed. It was no more that of a respectable personage moving about with dignity preoccupied with matters of state. It was now associated with a corrupt comic figure, surrounded by sycophants waiting for favours and the main chance.

I myself was an eyewitness to such a transformation of personality. An acquaintance of mine was suddenly made a cabinet minister. It came as a surprise to all of us who knew him. He was an indifferent social worker who had supposedly done some welfare work for his community. He was a high school drop-out. His father was a fuel depot owner living humbly in the back streets of his township. Our friend slipped into the role of a minister with alacrity. Very soon he was air-dashing all over the country, making speeches, cutting ribbons at inaugural functions and laying foundation stones. He would make a speech on any subject with a ring of authority. With equal ease, he would hold forth on our defence preparedness or the art of Bharatanatyam, caution against CIA espionage or eulogize about village handicrafts. His appearance changed. He began to look flabby. He kept away from his old friends and moved about encircled by bodyguards and secretaries. Rumours started circulating that he had become a millionaire through granting licences and permits. He had two cinema houses leased out, a three-star hotel, four bungalows rented to foreign companies in his wife's name, and controlled a few other profitable tit-bits.

Meanwhile those in his party high command were not ignorant about what was going on. They knew that ministers had made a lucrative job of their cabinet posts. The nation's urgent problems became a secondary matter.

Parliamentary debates became an uproarious carnival, with constant walkouts, shouting, thumping of desks, and marching to the well of the house. Marshals were being summoned to carry the unruly elements out of the house. From the press gallery I watched the sad spectacle of respectable, elderly citizens squabbling with each other over petty political matters. Once when the house was adjourned after such turmoil, without any business being transacted, I went to the main hall as I had done before to meet some of the MPs and ministers. But now I was stopped at the door and turned away. I brandished my press pass and said I always had access to the main hall. I tried to bluff my way in by saying that I rubbed shoulders with the MPs in the main hall even during the previous session. The man who stopped me said, 'It is written "Cartoonist" here on the card. And cartoonists are not allowed. Go and ask there.' He pointed to a large musty hall full of bundles of papers, files, tome-like ledgers lying all over the place stacked on benches, clerks, peons and hangers on. I approached the man near the door and explained my problem, repeating the lie that I had been permitted into the hall during the previous session. He took my card and examined it, adjusting the bifocals. Then he got up and wound his way through the tables, waste baskets and chairs to one of the numerous shelves in the remote corner. He pulled out a ledger. Flipping its pages, he traced his way back and replied, 'No, sir, you have not visited the hall since 1969. Rules were amended a few years ago and cartoonists are not allowed.'

I was naturally hurt and asked. 'Why?' He replied, 'Some cartoonist went in and drew caricatures of the MPs, that's why.' I left the room, filled with admiration for whatever department it was that could, in such chaotic conditions, keep track of my visits and was able to produce the proof within minutes!

The Janata government was edging towards the brink. The leaders thought a cabinet reshuffle would restore the vitality of the regime. But it only made things worse.

Mrs Gandhi was waiting in the wings to grab power, which she did eventually, riding on what was known as the 'Indira wave'. Shortly, some of those who had left the Congress and had floated a Congress party of their own with a different suffix, as well as others who had defected to other parties, trooped back saying sheepishly that they had been true Congressmen all their lives and that there was nothing to be ashamed of regarding rejoining the great Congress party.

Meanwhile Rajiv Gandhi was being requested by some senior leaders to to join the party. But he brushed them aside, saying he had nothing to do with politics. When further pressurized, he said he was quite happy to be a simple aeroplane pilot. Later when he joined the party he said he did not want any party post and was quite content to be just a party member. Still later, when he was asked to stand for elections from Amethi, he said he did not want to be elected to parliament from anywhere. When he was finally persuaded to stand for election, and won, he said he would not make a speech because he was not used to nor would he accept any cabinet or party post. I charted the progression of Rajiv's political career from airline pilot to national leader, frame by frame in a cartoon strip.

A few years later after the sudden and tragic assassination of Mrs Gandhi, Rajiv became the prime minister of India.

The moment I began to view him as the PM, I knew he would prove to be a difficult subject. He was tall, young and handsome. There was nothing in his physical features I could capture, exaggerate and exploit for my benefit. Nehru had a wonderful bald pate which I took the liberty of exposing, removing the Gandhi cap which he always wore. Mrs Gandhi, of course, had a great personality. But the wisp of lightning-like white hair she sported and the beak-like curve of her nose served my purposes.

Besides being a challenge to a caricaturist, Rajiv had ideas that were lofty, progressive, and of scientific temper. He wanted to take the country to an utopia located in the twenty-first century. I was worried that if he succeeded, I would lose my job. I would have a leader whose features I would not be able to distort and caricature, and I would be living in a country which would allow no scope for me to satirize and ridicule it.

Soon my hopes revived. I did not have to languish in a colourless utopia. The Congress (I) candidates for Lok Sabha elections were found to be star actors, dancers, celebrity sportsmen and so on. I was able to gather plenty of ideas from Rajiv's style of functioning. I even managed to find points in his features for distortion. I made him look a little more rotund than he really was, I shortened his nose and tilted it slightly upward. I thickened his eyebrows and reduced the hair on his pate, making him nearly bald. Thus having remodelled him to suit my purpose, I began to produce this image day after day for the *Times*. Shortly, people started to remark that Rajiv had begun to resemble my cartoon version of him, losing his original God-given good looks!

It was said that whenever any problem was brought to Rajiv's notice, he habitually answered, 'I will look into the matter.' It became a public joke to repeat this statement, even when there was no need to say so.

A coffee-table book, *The Eloquent Brush: A Selection*

of Cartoons from Nehru to Rajiv was published by the *Times of India* to commemorate its hundred and fiftieth year of publication. It was formally released by Rajiv Gandhi. Later that evening some of us were invited to tea with the prime minister. The guests were presented with a copy of my book. They kept these on a table in a corner of the hall, then proceeded to join the chief guest for tea. Rajiv was standing in the middle of the hall encircled by a small group of people eager to shake hands and chat with him. I was sitting in a chair and signing books for people who wanted my autograph. Someone saw me and invited me to meet the prime minister. I was led towards him and pushed through the ring of guests. He laughed in the usual way that people did when they met a cartoonist and said, 'I like your cartoons. But you make me look too fat.' Without batting an eyelid I replied spontaneously, 'I'll look into the matter,' raising knowing giggles and guffaws and sniggers all round.

After the party was over some of the guests came back into the empty hall, looking for their copies of *The Eloquent Brush* which they had left on the corner table. More than a dozen copies had vanished from there.

Earlier while autographing the books, I had noticed a very elegantly dressed lady who I was told was an important person in the PM's secretariat. She was flitting in and out of the hall. I was told later that she had squirreled away the books while their owners were clustering around Rajiv!

*

At about the same time I was invited by a group of

industrialists in Pune to be the chief guest at its annual get-together.

I arrived there early and checked into the hotel where a room had been booked for me. My host called and suggested we have beer and lunch, as the function would not begin till late in the evening.

We relaxed and chatted, sitting at the bar. The conversation followed the usual course—politics, corruption, the nuisance caused by VIP movement at the airports, pollution, traffic jams and so on. Then the subject turned to land prices, builders, rent, housing. And at that point I told my host I had a bungalow in Pune which I had bought years ago, but had neither lived in nor seen since I bought it. I had rented it out to a responsible company and it was being well maintained. He suggested that we go and see it the next morning.

We were still on our first beers, and the subject of our conversation was the bother and complication of owning immovable assets! I told him about an acre of farmhouse land I had bought in Bangalore many years ago and how luckily it slipped out of my hands, leaving far more money in my pocket than I had paid for it.

I told my host how once, on my way to Mysore from Bangalore, the chap who was accompanying me pointed to a patch of land just off the highway and said it was for sale. I would be wise to purchase it, he added.

I felt flattered and proud that I had been considered a prospective landlord! Soon I was blindly going through the formalities of drawing up an agreement, paying the money and signing the papers, visiting the registrar's office to get them stamped. And the unmarked acre of land became mine, in a vast field with some villages on the far horizon.

A few months later my friend asked for money to buy flagstones and barbed wire to fence the land off from the village, as the villagers were using it as a short cut to another village, grazing their cattle on my land and messing it up. I sent the money, and the land was secured within the barbed wire. Again another letter came to complain that the villagers were tampering with the fencing and stealing the flagstones. A watchman, therefore, was absolutely essential. Then I had to finance a little hut for him to stay in and keep vigil over the estate. I was getting worried about this property with its increasing problem of recurring expenses that it was generating. I was not directly in touch with these matters, but only through the friend with his explanation and demands, whatever these happened to be. Sitting in distant Bombay, I was in no position to question him. I was trying to avoid going to Bangalore to see for myself what was going on, fearing I would be further complicating my life. While I was puzzling over how to get rid of the land, flagstones, watchman, barbed wire and all, I heard a bit of hopeful news—the government was planning to acquire the land to implement their low-cost housing scheme. I was informed that the compensation would be pretty low. I did not care. I was in a mood to give the property away free.

At this moment my friend wrote to say that a builder was eager to buy the land, paying me a handsome advance. He would pay the balance after 'fixing' the minister concerned and the government officials in various offices for getting it exempted from the low-cost housing project. The advance, which was about four times the amount I had originally paid for the land, arrived promptly and I put it into the bank.

For several months there was no response from my friend. I sensed something shady about the transaction and was not sure my friend himself was not a party to it. I did not want to stick my neck out further into it asking questions. My whole concern now was to somehow wash my hands of the deal!

At last a letter arrived, reporting that the first buyer had retracted his offer because he did not have sufficient funds to influence the officials. The money given to me as an advance was not refundable legally, and therefore I could keep it! He went on to add that another estate developer was interested in the land and he would be remitting the advance soon. When this came, I was astonished that it was about twenty times more than what I had paid initially for that lucky acre of land in Bangalore!

All this happened many years ago. I have never heard from any of those people since. I told my host that years later I heard the land was finally acquired by the government.

We finished our beer and lunch and parted. In the evening the function went off smoothly. I made my speech, keeping the audience in stitches. I drew caricatures of leaders on large sheets of paper, which were auctioned and the money donated to charity.

The following morning, as agreed, my host picked me up to take me to have a look at my Pune bungalow, which I had not seen since I had bought it.

It was located in a posh area of the city, where industrialists and ministers lived. The acquiring of this property was a totally different experience from my Bangalore transaction years ago, I told my host.

This house had belonged to a high court judge. The person who negotiated the deal, prepared the legal documents, had the bungalow registered and so on, was a friend of the judge. He himself was an eminent lawyer. He made several trips from Pune to Bombay to complete the transaction. Finally the bungalow was mine.

Having bought it, I did not know what to do with it. At that time the chairman of a company, who was a very good friend, offered to take it on rent to accommodate one of his managers. Once again a very eminent lawyer of Bombay drew up the agreement, fixed the rent and added the proviso that the property should be well maintained, the garden tended, grass trimmed and the walls whitewashed once a year. Thus I was freed from the encumbrance of looking after the bungalow and the need to periodically visit and inspect it. So since the day I handed the tenant the keys, I had not gone to see it even once.

Now, driving around with my host in the area trying to locate my house, I lost my bearings. Over the years the area had developed and became unrecognizable, crowded with new apartments, bungalows, parks, gardens, avenues, trees. I went peering into each house that resembled my property. Finally I thought I saw it. The house was surrounded by a number of tall ashoka trees and bougainvillaea creepers. An expensive car was parked in the portico. It did not seem the house was mine. I took a chance, went into the compound and rang the bell. A man opened the door and looked questioningly at me. Since I did not know the tenant's name and had forgotten to read the nameplate on the gate I asked, 'Is this Laxman's house?' He replied, 'No, Laxman lives in Bombay,' and closed the door.

Driving back to the hotel, my host told me that it was a beautiful house no doubt, but I would need at least four servants to ensure my comfort—a watchman, a gardener, a bearer and a cook. It was not easy to get these. Besides, I would have to attend to everything myself—repair leaking pipes, service the water pump, fix the fuses and so on. He advised me to sell the property to a builder. It would fetch a good price, and I would also get a flat of my choice, designed to suit me. Necessities such as water, security, garden and so on would be taken care of by the housing society that would be formed.

Having thus recounted the story of my attempt at acquiring immovable property to a good listener, who paid undivided attention to my tale, I returned to Bombay. My friend's advice that I should sell the Pune bungalow was a very wise one, I thought, and I was determined to carry out the plan at the the first opportunity.

*

The next day I entered my office eagerly looking for letters, messages and telephone numbers which were usually piled on the table in my absence. To my disappointment, there were none except a few phone numbers written down by my peon, as if a beetle had crawled over the paper after climbing out of an ink well. I could hardly decipher them. There had been about six calls in my three days of absence. With great difficulty I managed to conclude they were all from the same party. I guessed that it must be for dinner or cocktails in honour of some foreign guest passing through the city in a hurry.

I decided to phone the person later in the day. I first wanted to settle down to do my work. I had read the paper for the last few days with scarcely any attention, and now I had to desperately search in the haystack of newspapers in front of me for two sharp needles to serve as ideas for my morning cartoon.

As was my habit, I put my legs up on the table and scoured each page, mulled over possible ideas, cogitating, pondering, contemplating, rejecting and choosing. After deciding on my subject, I weighed its potential relevance in the paper next day, visualizing its graphic possibilities. I mentally formulated the entire cartoon down to the carved legs of the furniture, if it happened to be that kind of setting, the pictures or graphs on the wall, the view outside the windows, the pattern on the curtains, the designs on the carpet, and last but not least—the clothes, stance and physical attributes of the politicians I was satirizing. Then came the punch line, full of self-importance and self-satisfaction mouthed by characters unaware that they were ridiculing themselves.

All this involved over four hours of intense concentration and mental torture. Now that I had settled on the idea, with great relief I began to fix the paper on my drawing board.

Just then the telephone rang. It was from a person with whom I had only a nodding acquaintance. He was an employee of an art centre which held exhibitions, seminars, music concerts and so on. He said he had called earlier when I was away to fix an appointment for a couple of journalists from the Philippines who were touring India and were eager to meet me. As usual I was initially reluctant and tried to avoid them. What had Filipino journalists got to do with me? The caller at the other end was waiting for my reply while I was debating whether to agree or not. I heard his voice. 'They are right here. If you are free I can ask them to go over to you straight away. They are leaving for Bangalore tomorrow . . .' I gave them an appointment for the following day.

Early the next morning the two journalists arrived. I was surprised to find that they were women! The fellow at the art centre had not told me this! They seemed elegant and delicate as butterflies. They spoke with the pleasant accent of all south-east Asians. The smiles on their faces never left. I made polite enquiries about their travels and how they were enjoying India, where else they proposed to go. They told me about their visit to Agra and how they were struck by the grandeur of the Taj Mahal. They said they were now on the way to south India to get an impression of places of interest there.

Then they asked me about my work. I mechanically narrated my biography, having given such interviews many times before. They took notes and asked the standard question I find impossible to answer—how did I get the ideas for my cartoons?

On the whole I enjoyed their presence in my room. They did not bother me with too many questions, and left quietly soon afterwards.

Meanwhile I began to plan an exhibition of my crows. I drew them one after another in various postures—on branches of trees, sitting on the edge of an earthen pot, in flight, in flocks and perched on TV cables, neatly like scores on a music sheet. In between the working on the crow sketches, I wrote short stories and travelogues and edited another collection of *You Said It* cartoons.

At this time, the theme for my second novel was germinating at the back of my mind. I did not sit down to write it, But I immensely enjoyed thinking over the plot at odd moments, when I was waiting in the airport lounge, or in bed after switching off the light, or in prolonged traffic jams. The characters of the novel took shape, developed and faded away sometimes. All this helped to free my mind from the routine national political events. For several months I let the plot remain as it was. But the hero had a concrete identity. He was an ambitious young man assisting in bringing out a magazine called *The Messenger*. The proprietor was a shady fellow using the magazine as a front for many nefarious activities. The other characters remained hazy and I did not know what course the story would take.

One day my peon handed me a telex message as I entered the room. It read, 'We are pleased to inform you that you have been chosen for the Ramon Magsaysay Foundation Award. Letter follows with further details.'

Quite a few of my colleagues indulged in practical jokes, and I knew the fake telex was from one of them. Nevertheless I showed it to one of the senior members of the editorial department. He examined it, and I was surprised he did not laugh as I expected. At that moment the news editor entered the room waving a report from PTI. 'R.K. Laxman, the cartoonist of the *Times of India*, has been honoured with the prestigious Magsaysay Award for professional excellence . . .'

From that moment on I was flooded with phone calls and telegrams congratulating me. When I went home I found my drawing room like a florist's shop.

But I was sorry my wife was not present to share the excitement and the joy of this unexpected international honour. She was away on a tour of Europe and America with some of her friends. I did not know where exactly she was at the moment all this was happening to me. I had no way of phoning her or sending a cable to give her the good news.

Then messages came from the Foundation about arrangements for our travel to the Philippines, accommodation, details of our programmes on arrival, photo sessions, press interviews and so on.

I waited anxiously for my wife. She was due to arrive any day, and she would be left with just enough time to pack and accompany me to the Philippines.

A couple of days later she phoned from the airport to say she was back, and asked if it was a fact that I had won the Magsaysay Award. Apparently the immigration officials, upon seeing her passport, asked if she was the wife of the cartoonist who had won the award. Since she had just arrived and had no idea that I had won the prize, she requested the official for the use of the phone to call me. I confirmed the good news. She said she would be home after her baggage was cleared.

I waited for hours, but there was no sign of her. I phoned the airport, but I could not get much help from anyone there. For hours I stared out of the window, waiting for her taxi.

At last it arrived. I hurried my servant down to carry her luggage. I was surprised to see her walk straight into the house without any bags! She said they had got lost somewhere at Kennedy airport in New York or at Heathrow in London.

Apart from her own personal items, they contained a

lot of gifts for friends and relatives. But the sense of loss was soon forgotten because of the thrill of our imminent departure for the Philippines to collect my fabulous award!

The aircraft landed at Manila and taxied towards the ramp. From the window I saw groups of people with bouquets in hand, awaiting the arrival of the awardees. Welcome banners fluttered in the wind. Winners were arriving from various parts of Asia—Japan, India, Indonesia, and so on.

My wife and I walked to the lounge, shaking hands with people who had come to receive us, accepting the offerings of flowers, waving to the groups of cheering people. After the formal introduction to the trustees of the Foundation and the ritual exchange of pleasantries, we were escorted to the car that was to drive us to our hotel.

Just as I was about to get into it, two ladies walked up to me, flashing bright smiles which seemed curiously familiar. 'Probably you don't recognize us,' one of them said giggling. I was nonplussed and began to rake my memory, staring at them steadily for clues. Then the setting began to form; it was a morning in the *Times of India* office nearly a year ago; two women journalists touring India at that time were calling on me. As soon as the fragments of that scene fell into place, recognition dawned! With a hoop of joy, I shook hands with them and introduced them to my wife as journalists from the Philippines who had called on me in Bombay. One of them interrupted me, saying they were no journalists but officials of the Magsaysay Foundation. As soon as I had been tentatively selected for the award, they were sent to India under the guise of journalists to assess my worthiness to receive the honour. This mission had taken them to Bangalore, where they called on some of my old friends and college professors to find out more about me, engaging them in seemingly casual conversation. When they were in Bombay they had visited the bookshops to collect my *You Said It* books, and chatted with the proprietors to extract more information about the author.

I was astonished to learn about the trouble they had taken and the extent of the spadework they had done to qualify me for the award. Similar teams had been sent to Japan to research the background of an engineer, a priest in Sri Lanka, a professor in Indonesia, an economist in Bangladesh.

Before the award ceremony we were measured for a special kind of traditional shirt, exclusively tailored and given to us to be worn on the occasion. The function went off with quiet dignity and each of the recipients had to make a short acceptance speech. I thanked the Magsaysay Award Committee for selecting me for the award, and in a lighter vein I described the importance of humour and laughter in a worry-ridden world. I said the award should be really shared with all those who make my profession worthwhile, namely the rulers—bureaucrats at various administrative levels, and the politicians. I heard satisfying ripples of laughter as I concluded my speech.

The following days were spent in attending cocktails and dinners and visiting tourist spots in Philippines. During this time I became quite friendly with the economist from Bangladesh. He told me a lot of stories about the rule under Pakistan, the struggle for liberation, the war with India, the entry of the Indian Army and finally the creation of Bangladesh.

*

When he was narrating all this, I was reminded of my own experiences during that time on the border of East Pakistan and India.

I was then in Calcutta, invited by some organization to deliver a talk. War was about to break out between the two nations. Refugees were pouring into Bengal from across the border. I wanted to visit some of the refugee camps and do some sketches for our paper. A reporter from our Calcutta office accompanied me to the sites. I had never imagined the plight of the refugees would be so horrifying. Makeshift tents were pitched in a vast field, and their number seemed pathetically inadequate to cope with the flood of refugees arriving every minute. I heard hair-raising cries and moans on all sides. It was sad to see people rush towards our car as it bounced its way over the rough ground. We were mistaken for some government agency bringing them desperately needed succour. As we got down from the car and walked, the refugees followed us, crying and pleading for help.

A number of straw mats rolled up like bedding were lying all over the place. I did not realize what they were till I saw, to my horror, a pair of feet sticking out of one of them. The bundles were corpses awaiting disposal. Some doctors were moving about among the refugees, giving injections, administering medicine, feeling pulses and so on. I saw a man fall to one side and expire just as the doctor was examining him!

My sense of horror and shock at the extent of human misery and suffering settled down to a deep depression as we walked back to the car. Sitting inside, I somehow managed to make a few sketches.

We drove in silence, benumbed by the sight we had seen. The car moved on, humming steadily over what seemed to be a trunk road. Slowly we began to talk about the political implications of the situation and the imminent threat of war between India and Pakistan. I saw glimpses of soldiers' encampments in open fields, army trucks, jeeps and guns. After a while we were lost in our discussion. Now and then I glanced at the straight road ahead, lined with trees. The driver accelerated, as there were no signs of pedestrians, traffic or cattle.

Then I saw a man crossing the road in the far distance. The driver did not slow down, expecting the man to move to the other side. But no! The man took up position in the middle of the road, facing the car. As we slowed down we saw that he was a soldier in battle dress, aiming his rifle at us. He ordered us to get out of the vehicle, and menacingly directed us to walk to a hut in the middle of a rice field. My attempt to talk to him produced no response. He had a dark expressionless face with a fierce moustache curling upwards. Gun in hand, he brought up the rear as he marched the three of us single file across the paddy field to the hut. I thought we had been taken prisoner by the Pakistan army, and that we were finished. Inside the hut an army officer was sitting at a table examining a large map. He looked tired and viewed us through eyes that were dull and red from a lack of sleep. He asked in a guttural voice what we were doing in that area. We said we were journalists from Bombay visiting the refugee camps.

'Don't you know you are in a prohibited zone? This is Jessore Road, leading straight to Pakistan. If you had gone on for another five minutes you would have entered enemy territory, been taken prisoner and shot!' I was relieved that we were not Pakistani prisoners and these were our own men. I apologized and told the officer that we did not know the area was out of bounds, that no one had told us so, nor had anyone stopped us. 'Where were you heading, anyway?' he asked. I turned to the reporter, who blinked and looked back at me! We had left it to the driver to conduct us through the area, and thought he was taking us to some more refugee camps. We explained this to the officer and appealed to him to let us off.

He looked at us angrily and roared, 'Do you hear that?' At that moment there were terrifying explosions outside. 'Shells from Pakistan are being fired on our territory. In a few days we expect a bloody war between the two countries, and here you are merrily driving into Pakistan as if you are invited to a picnic there!' he shouted, pounding the table with his fist.

He picked up the phone, spoke into it and listened for a long time. Then he turned to us and said, 'You are not telling the truth! Your driver being questioned in the next hut informs us that you are businessmen from Calcutta, not journalists from Bombay. I am afraid I can't let you go till the matter is investigated.' With hopeless finality he turned his back on us, began looking at his maps and taking notes.

I panicked at the sudden turn of events. Here I was fearing, at first, that I was a prisoner of the Pakistanis, and now I had become, ironically, a prisoner of India! I desperately asked if I could telephone my office in Calcutta and prove we were journalists. Without turning to us he said, 'No. The army's field telephone can't be used for civilian purposes, sorry.'

We both sat in a corner for several hours quietly like two schoolchildren undergoing punishment.

What was going to be our ultimate fate? How was this tragicomedy to end? Who would come over to this vast, desolate corner of Bengal to redeem us, I wondered.

The officer turned towards us at last, moved by our total silence. 'OK, I will let you off now. Just jump into your vehicle and scoot straight to where you belong. No turning this side or that side or halting on the way! Understood?' 'Yes, sir!' We scrambled into the car and left for Calcutta.

On the way we asked the driver why did he have to tell them we were from Calcutta? Because he thought so, he said! How was he to know? He was a Bihari and new to Calcutta, not familiar with its places and people.

After this nerve-racking incident I flew back to Bombay and plunged straight into my work, producing cartoons like a factory on the Indo-Pak war day after day. I could not think of any other theme as it would seem out of place in an atmosphere surcharged with talk of the ongoing war.

Finally our troops triumphed. The Indian government agreed on a neutral zone in Dacca for the formal Pakistani surrender, and reserved the Hotel Intercontinental as a safe shelter for civilians and foreign diplomats. I did a cartoon as a finale, which appeared in the morning edition. I depicted a battered and wounded President Yahya Khan in the process of packing up and fleeing, phoning and asking, 'Is that the Hotel Intercontinental? Well, I would like a reservation . . .'

After the war hysteria blew over I resumed my normal activity of lampooning our national political leaders, puncturing their egos and distorting their images, regardless of whether they were in the ruling party or in the opposition.

Although I enjoyed my work and applied myself to it almost compulsively, at the back of my mind I always nurtured plans to get away from it all every now and then.

I thought of going on a trip to Rajasthan, which I had not visited so far. My wife and I spread out a map and a tourist brochure one day, and sat down to work out our tour of the desert land. We had even fixed our date of departure when a letter arrived from the postal apprising department. It informed me that I had been held guilty of importing obscene literature into the country in violation of the Sea Customs Act of 1892, Section II. I was further told that the offensive material had been impounded and I was ordered to explain why I should not be prosecuted!

As I read it an ice-cold chill went down my spine! I later learnt that a well-meaning American friend, who was posted at the US consulate in Bombay years earlier, had sent me the bumper issue of *Playboy* magazine as a Christmas gift.

I began to run around desperately looking for trusted friends who would help me out of this embarrassing situation. But instead of helping me, after reading the letter quizzically as if I had been caught in some naughty act, they asked in a confiding tone if I would let them have a look at the forbidden magazine!

I spent sleepless nights searching for a solution to this inadvertent mess. Not finding any, I decided in despair to ask the postal authority itself for a way out. An officer of the department suggested that if I was really innocent, I should say so in a letter, plead total ignorance of the matter and disown any knowledge of the sender, my American friend!

I promptly drafted the letter according to his instructions, and handed it over to him.

Days and weeks passed, but there was no response from the postal department. I had expected an immediate reply pronouncing me innocent and acquitting me honourably.

Gradually with the passing of time my anxiety wore off. I even began to regale groups of friends at parties with this story, which kept them roaring with laughter.

This comic interlude had disrupted our plans for a holiday in Rajasthan. Once I regained my mood to go on the trip, I rapidly completed all the arrangements for our departure.

Through heat and blinding glare we drove on in our car. The sun kept its intensity of heat unvarying from dawn to dusk. The road on the yellow desert sand stretched in an unending straight course. There was no greenery around except the occasional cluster of nondescript desert creepers and cacti.

The terrain was bleak, parched and drab! So it seemed! But our initial impression was wrong. Paradoxically the landscape was indeed dabbed with a variety of colours when looked at keenly: the women of Rajasthan in ethnic multi-coloured finery as they flitted about to fetch water or gathered firewood for cooking, and men in blazing red turbans leading their majestic camels heaven knew where to in that vast sheet of desert. I was further intrigued by the colourful birds including peacocks cheerfully gambolling on the desert sand. Even the stones and rocks contributed colour. There were snow-white marble stones, yellow granite and stones red as unbaked brick. All these dotted the whole region in the buildings, temples, majestic palaces of kings and their mighty fortresses.

Thoroughly refreshed by our three-week sojourn in Rajasthan away from newspapers and political gossip, I returned to Bombay.

My plan was to make colour drawings from some of the sketches I had made of Rajasthani camels, havelis, fortresses, women in ghagras, street musicians and so on. I wanted to start on these immediately and send them to a magazine which always welcomed any work from me. But on my table I saw a pile of letters—from relatives and friends, invitation cards, bills. Among them was a sickly-brown envelope bearing a Government of India stamp. My heart missed a beat at the sight of correspondence from the postal department. I did not realize that I was still held guilty of impunities committed under the Sea Customs Act; I had supposedly imported obscene literature into the country over a year ago!

I hurriedly tore open the envelope and read the letter, skimming over the chilling words, anxious to get to the vital point where my punishment was pronounced. '. . . penal . . . action . . . *Playboy* . . . objectionable goods . . . Customs Act . . . 1892 . . .' Just as I was about to resign myself to being jailed as an obscene-minded freak in a community of people of high morals, I saw typed faintly at the very bottom of the letter, 'Your explanation has been accepted and the offending material has been seized absolutely.' Thereby meaning that I had been honourably acquitted!

This unexpected news boosted my spirits. I began to prepare the colour drawings of Rajasthan.

While I was working on these it occurred to me, quite unrelated to the subject I was tackling, that I should have an exhibition of my crow drawings. I had always looked at crows with fascination and considered them the best among birds. Even as a child I had watched them for hours and sketched them in various poses. They had a colour which stood out boldly against any background. As I grew up I realized that crows had a temperament close to that of humans—clever, cunning and cautious! Above all one could spot them any time of the day to study and draw in all sorts of postures and moods: on tree branches, near the garden tap, on the window sill, perching on TV antennae and rooftops, and in flight across the blue sky. I found crows ubiquitous, and engagingly active. Besides in our mythology and folk tales this bird's involvement was recounted frequently.

I learned further details about this bird when I visited the Smithsonian Institute in Washington, DC. The museum's research on crows had shown that they passed most intelligence tests, and could count up to seven objects!

I held my first crow exhibition in Madras and Bombay. For most viewers my work came as a revelation. They discussed it with surprising vehemence, as if they had not seen a crow before.

A few years later I held a similar crow exhibition. But this time out of the twenty-one pictures I usually exhibited, I presented only ten crows along with twelve paintings of Ganapati.

The concept of this deity had always interested me. I found its physical shape endearing, and in the labyrinth of my subconscious mind there had been a constant effort to resolve all sights and shapes, no matter how tenacious, remote, vague or abstract, into this dynamic form. From the rocky contour of a distant hill to a tiny shrivelled seed, from the gnarled root of a wild shrub to the twisted and tangled droops of a banyan tree or the three-cornered leaf of a potted plant—by a little push to one's imagination one could immediately perceive the rotund figure with chubby limbs, flapping ears, trunk and all! This god was present but not immediately visible in a colossal tree, vaguely manifest in a wisp of drifting cloud, in ancient boulders casually lying around for geological ages at a mountainside. I rendered my fancies in odd combinations that evoked the deity's playful character and astonishing, eccentric power. These portrayals, along with my realistic black crows, interested, intrigued and fascinated those who came to see the exhibition.

Soon there were quite a few who wanted pictures of crows or of Ganapati to hang on their walls at home, or to give away as gifts to friends and relatives. The demand did not intimidate me. I found it very relaxing to draw crows after returning home in the evening, having dealt with political events.

The diversion I sought in painting crows and Ganapati, however, was only in the evening at home and on holidays. I anxiously ensured that it did not interfere in any way with my daily business of producing political cartoons, and the spartan discipline that I observed in my work.

But many who belong to my fraternity take it very easy. The time devoted to their professional work seems incidental to their more relaxing preoccupations. Of course, cartoons of the kind one sees in magazines and columns devoted to provoking a smile need less exacting concentration—for instance, funny situations arising out of helpless parents dealing with a naughty boy, or the driver of a speeding car caught by the police, or a fat lady trying to lose weight, or humour arising from doctor-patient relations, bungling players on the golf course, situations in cocktail parties, and so on. Several variations of all these could be drawn and stashed away and the cartoonist could relax till the stock lasted.

But not so the political cartoonist. He has to be alert and wrestle with the political events as and when they arise, and he should prove worthy of his reputation day after day. I used to look upon some of the cartoonists with secret wonder—how could they be loitering when the sword of the deadline to produce the cartoon was hanging over their heads!

When I was in England I knew a cartoonist who always came to the Press Club after a good game of golf on a sunny day. He would have a sumptuous lunch accompanied by drinks, and dally over them for hours. Then he would amble out of the club, mumbling that he had to rush to his office. And his cartoon unfailingly appeared in the morning paper. I felt somewhat ashamed for flogging myself from 8.30 a.m. to 5.00 p.m. at my drawing board, allowing no visitors or telephone calls while I remained in a state of trance waiting for an idea! Looking at my friends' methodologies, I felt there was some secret trick or formula to this art, which I had failed to learn to make my task easier!

There was another cartoonist who belonged to a prestigious British daily who could not do without going riding during the best part of the normal working hours, when he ought to have been sharpening his wits in his studio, puncturing the bloated egos of his leaders and showering ridicule on them.

I met a dog lover who also happened to be a cartoonist. He lived in a country house in the suburbs of London. He never went to the office but sent his cartoons by courier every day. Observing his lifestyle, I was amazed that he was able to do any work let alone draw cartoons! He was surrounded by half a dozen dogs of various breeds all the time and was engaged in bathing and brushing them, taking the whole pack for walks, or running through nearby fields to exercise his pets. Later he fed them and put them to bed! And yet there it was—his cartoon in the morning's paper.

A cartoonist in America was so well paid for his work that he was able to indulge in his favourite hobby—flying his own private plane. He kept hopping from place to place wherever a baseball match was on. Of course, these cartoonists did not rise to great heights in their profession. Nevertheless they were able to satisfy their ambition to be cartoonists, and combine this with their desire to indulge in a carefree pastime of their choice.

Nearer home too I had seen a few editorial cartoonists lounging in coffee-house chairs, in sofas at clubs, at the swimming pool or at the bar, at odd hours. Of course, that might be the idea for the cartoon being fed by the editor or some witty editorial staff. In such cases the cartoonist was left with a lot of free time. His job was simply to illustrate another man's ideas.

It was in Perth, Australia that I came across a cartoonist who, his professional competence apart, had achieved something working in his spare time as a diversion that earned my admiration.

He had just finished his work for the day when I met him in his office. He suggested a quiet dinner at his home. I jumped at the idea. We drove in his car to his house in the suburbs. It was a large red-brick building with a neatly laid garden, garage and swimming pool. The spacious sitting room had a well-stocked bar in a corner. The furnishing and decor were tasteful. His wife hovered around with glasses, snacks and the ice bucket. We perched on barstools and chatted generally about world affairs, discussed our professions, travel experiences, and so on. In the course of the conversation I looked around casually and complimented him on his nice house. Immediately he perked up and shouted, 'Jenny!' to his wife, who had gone into the kitchen. 'Laxman here likes our house!' She shouted back, 'Does he now? Isn't that wonderful?'

I was surprised that my casual remark had provoked such excitement! It was a simple compliment which could have been acknowledged with a polite smile. But here my host climbed down from the stool with great exuberance and poured a generous round of drinks, announcing, 'We built this house!' What was so great about that, I wondered! Everyone who could afford it built his own house! He saw the lack of surprise on my face and said, 'Jenny and I built this house brick by brick with our own hands. We drew up the plan, dug the foundation, baked the bricks . . . during that time we lived in that garage, where I have put my car now.' He went on to tell me that returning from the office after giving the day's cartoon, he and his wife worked until late at night constructing the house with the help of powerful floodlights fixed to poles. It gave them great joy to see the building grow literally brick by brick. Then he took me around the garden and pointed out various trees and plants he had planted himself, and the swimming pool which he had dug singlehandedly, fixed tiles at the bottom and filled with water. 'We swim every day before dinner,' he said, flicking a switch on the wall. Immediately the entire pool glowed blue with submerged lights!

The cartoonist group in the Soviet Union bore the stamp of the Communist system they were living in. The cartoonist I was introduced to belonged to a famous satirical weekly called *Krokodile*. Its cartoons were meticulously drawn with great academic perfection, and were visually amusing. But the satire uniformly consisted of attacks on anonymous enemies of the Republic such as laziness at factory sites; red tape; bureaucracy; waste of precious utilities such as water, power and so on. And, of course, cartoons liberally illustrated the vulgarity of capitalism and the cruelty of imperialism. They never touched on the real issues and real people in the Union. The cartoons were products of collective effort and discussion.

I was introduced to a dozen cartoonists sitting around a table in the office of the *Krokodile*. We were given mugs of coffee and we viewed each other, grinning without uttering a word. I was handicapped by my ignorance of the language, and there was no interpreter. The meeting was conducted mostly in silence except for murmured exchanges and occasional laughter. Seeing that I was isolated, one of them mustered all the knowledge he had of English and after a great deal of gesturing and consulting with his colleagues, put his question haltingly, 'How much salary you are paid by your office?'

Although China was under Communism, I found the cartoonists there lively and talkative. I was astonished to find numerous cartoonist clubs and associations. One of the visiting cards given to me read, *Editing Board Member, Satire and Humour, Cartoonists Association of China.* Another card carried the information, *Member of Editorial*

Board, World of Cartoons.

But here as in Russia, cartoons ridiculed in a general way the slowness of government procedure, red tape, neglect of civic duties and so on. I found the draftsmanship to be uniformly weak and stereotyped. There was no touch of visual humour. Cartoons seemed to belong more to the family of calligraphy, an art in which the Chinese excelled.

I had an unforgettable experience watching a master of calligraphy demonstrate his superb skills. A cartoonist association had arranged for a demonstration in my hotel in Beijing. The calligrapher was a genial-looking man with a soft snow-white beard and ever-smiling eyes. He went around bowing and shaking hands as we drank little cups of tea. When we were ready to see the demonstration, he took from his bag a large brush and a palette to mix the black paint in. He rolled a white sheet of rice paper on the table.

We watched all his movements in expectant silence. He studied the paper with piercing eyes, holding the brush poised to attack the white sheet. He took a couple of steps back, stood still, then suddenly lunged forward, dipped the brush in the pool of black paint in the palette, and quickly made a deep black stroke at the top of the paper all in one go. Then he stood back, smiling. The hushed silence gave way to appreciative laughter. Then again he suddenly moved, dipped the brush in the ink and without a pause rapidly moved the brush criss-cross over the paper as if to silent music that only he could hear. But it infected my cartoonist friends who swayed and clapped rhythmically as the calligrapher's hand went on moving vertically down the paper putting in those enchanting strokes. It ultimately communicated to me also as his brush journeyed leaving in its wake the most enchanting pattern of Chinese characters. He filled up the whole sheet and we all clapped as he concluded his symphony and gave him an ovation in one voice as though we had listened to a most rapturous concert.

I examined his creation. I noted that he had dribbled the ink from the brush in certain places on the paper, while barely touching certain other parts. He had slashed some areas with bold strokes here and there. On the whole it was visual music. Finally he rolled the paper up neatly, tied it with a silk ribbon and presented it to me. I thanked him and the organizers profusely and asked what the calligrapher's message was. There was a twitter of laughter among the gathering. I was told it meant, 'A warm welcome to China, comrade Laxman'. I was delighted, and replied that the function could not end without my giving something in return, expressing my gratitude to the artist and the association.

I took out a roll of rice paper, spread it on the table just as he had and imitated his stance, much to the amusement of the gathering. I held the brush aloft, suddenly dipped the brush in the ink and moved it swiftly over the paper writing the message. I heartily thanked the cartoonist's association for their warm welcome. I wrote in English script in mock-Chinese style vertically. Then I drew my Common Man with his striped coat and famous bewildered look.

It struck me that most of the world's cartoonists would rather do something other than draw cartoons, at the same time not sacrificing the status of a cartoonist. I had seen them rear puppies, build houses brick by brick, fly about in single-engine aeroplanes, ride horses and so on. Perhaps there were cartoonists who explored the ocean bed and climbed insurmountable peaks. I had no opportunity to meet them.

The Japanese cartoonist I met was on the staff of the largest national daily. The newspaper building was a massive labyrinth of endless corridors. The staff rushed about, tense with the effort of meeting their deadlines, since several editions came out each day.

He was a thin, middle-aged man. He had wrinkles permanently imprinted on his face at the right places giving him a tranquil look. He asked the usual questions—how long I had been in Japan, how long I proposed to stay there, how I liked it and so on. I got the impression that the deadline for his cartoon was fast approaching, and I was in his way. So I got up, giving some excuse about another engagement, and took his leave. He requested me to come to his other office the following day, and bring some of my own work so he could have a look.

The next morning I was sitting in his room in another part of Tokyo. I had taken cartoon samples featuring Nehru, Indira, Rajiv. Just as I was explaining the satirical content to my companion, I was shaken by a shattering noise coming from the floor above. But my friend remained cool and continued to ask questions about my method of work, the material I used etc. As I began to answer him, the deafening explosion reccured. But the cartoonist remained unmoved. I could hardly concentrate on what he was saying, since all my attention and my nerves were geared to receive the next bout of explosion which occured at uneven intervals.

After a while the cartoonist got up and invited me to follow him. He took me to the upper floor where we entered a vast hall with a wooden floor and no furniture. People were sitting along the wall. They all stood up the moment they saw the cartoonist and bowed with great reverence. Then he led me to a reserved space on the floor. I sat down next to him. I noticed everyone present was in some kind of uniform.

The crowd settled down and a hush fell. The cartoonist clapped his hands, beckoned to someone and told him something in Japanese. That man went around, selected a short fellow and made him take up a position in the middle of the hall. Then he signaled to a tall American to stand up. Suddenly he shouted something, and the American charged like a frenzied bull towards the short man, as if to seize him and tear him to bits. Before I was able to realize what was happening, the short chap had picked up the American with the ease of a ballet dancer and hurled him to the floor with a great thud and stood over him without any expression of triumph on his face. This was the explosive noise I had kept hearing in the cartoonist's room downstairs!

For my benefit the American was requested to attack the chap half his size, from all angles and using various techniques. Each time the American was repulsed, and he flew through the air and fell down again and again.

The cartoonist explained that this was an art of defence like karate. But it was called Aikido. The cartoonist was a grandmaster and designated high priest of this art, and the place it was taught was called the temple. This grandmaster supervised three such temples in Japan. He visited them in turn, spending a week in each to teach, correct and polish the art of self-defence to perfection. Thus he devoted only one week a month to cartooning.

For all the power and skill he wielded as a grandmaster, his draftsmanship was rather anaemic. I found his illustrations spidery and without vitality. Maybe he packed all his humour and satirical punch into the captions!

I sat back and wondered whether, judging from what I saw in the world of cartooning, this art was not on its way out gradually. Whether in the East or in the West it seemed to be in a state of decline.

Viewers appeared to be satisfied with mere doodles passed off as cartoons carrying the labels such as UN, WB, PM, USA, DMK, CONG, BJP, and so on. If the reader failed to understand the cartoon, he modestly assumed that he had a limited knowledge of current politics. If he did catch the central concept, he wondered if he was missing some subtle satire. Some cartoonists dashed off a sketch without caring for the draftsmanship, which after all was essential for visual humour. There were others whose draftsmanship was so painstakingly stylized and elaborate that it virtually stood in the way of communicating the main idea to the reader. Quite a few cartoonists got away by re-illustrating old ideas or copying someone else's work unbashedly.

Added to all this the invasion of cartoons produced with the help of computers further eroded the quality of this art. The device seemed to show an easy way out eliminating the labour of drawing. Cartoons created by these mechanical means by cartoonists with or without talent had no individuality, they looked stereotypical and utterly soulless!

The politician, usually the one who inspired the cartoons, had also a share in lowering the quality of cartoons. Earlier his political cunning, the deception he practised on the gullible public without being caught, the false promises he made during election time, were all material for the cartoonist. He exposed these hidden characteristics through his cartoons, giving a moment of joy to the tormented common man. But over the years, the sinister motives and evil intentions of the politicians ceased to be subtle. They became transparent as if put in a glass case for all to see. The cartoonist needed to do nothing to expose or reveal the clown behind the mask!

A politician shaking hands with an underworld gangster holding a suitcase full of currency notes was no longer an improbable or outrageous sight. And it was no secret at all that an impostor, in the guise of a bearded godman with holy ash splattered all over his forehead, was advising and guiding the prime minister in the matter of laundering the kickbacks from foreign deals and helping him to put them in numbered Swiss bank accounts. The whole affair was a caricature in itself, if viewed with a sense of humour. There was no need for a cartoonist.

Another ridiculous aspect of our democratic system was that proven gangsters, murderers and smugglers could enter politics freely and stand for elections from behind bars, to represent the people and serve them. Once again, like so many other such comical characteristics, one could laugh one's heart out by just reading the item on the paper, without the good offices of the cartoonist.

Similarly, news about scams, corruption, defection, party splits, infighting, CBI investigations and judicial enquiries that one read in the paper, were all carbon copies of what had happened yesterday and the day before and would happen tomorrow and the day after, and the day after that. Repetitive, tedious and predictable. There was no opportunity to make a cartoon scintillating and brilliant day after day. The apparent abundance of ideas spewed out by the political leaders for the benefit apparently of the cartoonist were really of no help at all to him, as was popularly believed. It was nerve-racking to read almost the same news, assimilate, analyse and create a cartoon with fresh brilliance day after day.

But what saved the cartoonist was the insatiable appetite of the public to enjoy denigrating and pillorying its leaders in several variations, even if the situation happened to be the same.

In a somewhat gloomy mood I pondered the future of my profession. It was clearly entering a painful period. But I hoped that my strict observance of routine and discipline in my work would see me through the unrelenting daily grind till the time came to enjoy my happy and well-earned retirement!

But just as I was indulging in pessimistic reflections, an offer came my way which, if I had been tempted enough to accept, would have shattered my zealously-guarded work ethic and put an end to my career as a political cartoonist!

While browsing through the volumes of my *You Said It* books, a documentary filmmaker got the bright idea that a movie could be made out of my cartoons! The producer was a lady who had been very successful in this branch of cinema. When she suggested her new idea I recoiled, saying I could never undertake the project. I rejected it outright. In the first place I had no experience in this field, except a brief period decades ago in a Madras studio, trying to make a cartoon film. There I had observed the methods and habits of people in this field, and developed a strong prejudice. They seemed to take things extremely casually, never bothering about punctuality in keeping appointments. They dallied over cups of coffee and snacks for hours which they called 'conferences' and 'discussions' about the project on hand.

The producer persisted and wanted to know what I thought of the idea, regardless of whether I took up the work or not. She told me that the plot was to be based broadly on the life of my Common Man. It was to be a series of episodes related to his day-to-day experiences—catching the city bus or train to go to the office, standing in a queue in front of a ration shop, coping with diminishing water in the bathroom tap, and so on. After this description the producer looked at me as if expecting me to fill in the rest of the relevant details. I answered that my Common Man was not real. He had never uttered a word in all his life. It would look odd if his lips moved and he talked in a film. But in the back of my mind I was already considering alternatives. How to use the plot without the presence of my Common Man? It seemed a challenging task. I was fascinated by the idea of creating a film version of my *You Said It* cartoons.

Soon I was involved in producing the episodes. But I put forward several conditions before I accepted the assignment. These were strange demands, from the point of view of traditional film production.

I said I would not put pen to the paper to write the script. I would not direct the film in a studio. I would select the actors myself after testing their abilities. The producer was good enough to agree to all my conditions, the purpose of which was to protect my hours of office work, so I could complete my daily cartoons without interference by the film work.

I used to finish my work at the *Times* in the evening and drive straight to the producer's house. In the drawing room there would already be a gathering of actors, script writers, directors. I used to be carried away while describing the story. I made it so vivid as if it was a real happening in my life. I used to put in a lot of acting, mimicry, facial expressions while telling the story. I felt that my audience in the room listened and watched me spellbound as though they were viewing a film.

I had always held the opinion that people turned a blind eye to their environment and failed to notice ordinary facts. The two dozen episodes I churned out for the producer were all just trivial daily incidents in anyone's life—taps suddenly running dry in the bathrooms, admitting a boy to school, hiring a new servant, a distant relative suddenly arriving as a guest, and so on. It was directed by a fully qualified professional in a regular studio, and this man knew what I wanted of the actors. The dialogue was based on my tape-recorded narration. Finally I used to see the video of the episode and suggest editing and correction based on it. Eventually the film was shown on Doordarshan. It was a great success. The producer wanted more. I tossed off thirteen episodes effortlessly. But nothing came of these, as our producer was not keen on bribing the necessary peons, clerks and bureaucrats in the ministry to get the official approval for the production.

Thus I dabbled in the art of filmmaking for some time. The satisfaction I derived from it was that I did it in my own unorthodox way. Otherwise it needed the talent of too many hands to create a successful film. This kind of sustained cooperative endeavour did not appeal to my ego as an individual artist.

*

Now that I was free except for my routine work for the *Times*, the thought of my flat in Pune, fully furnished and equipped but lying vacant, began to bother me. Years earlier I had taken the advice of my friends, sold my bungalow and purchased a flat in its place. At that time everyone had told me it would be a great problem to evict an old tenant. It would involve dealing with lawyers, law courts, adjournments, petitions and counter-petitions for months on end. In a way I was secretly happy, because I would not have to look for a builder if the tenant refused to leave. Having started the process, I wrote a formal letter to the industrial company I had rented my bungalow to, asking them to leave.

But to my astonishment, just a fortnight later the manager phoned to say the bungalow had been vacated and that I was free to take possession of it whenever I wished to do so. Within a week of my receiving the house keys, a builder appeared at my office in Bombay. The deal for the sale was struck. I had sold the Pune bungalow in no time!

From then on everything moved smooth and fast. Before I realized it my flat was ready, built according to our plans. My wife and I stood in the middle of the vast empty apartment, marvelling at its size and appointments. Our housing complex consisted of two blocks, each with four flats. It was surrounded by a modest garden. It was called Iris Park.

We went to a dealer in the market and placed orders for a refrigerator, an airconditioner, a vacuum cleaner, a cooking range and a washing machine, and had these put in working order in our flat the same day. The following morning I had the telephone installed. Then we went to a furniture shop and placed the order for a dining table, chairs, sofa sets and beds, all made of cane.

A few weeks later again we drove up to Pune with a few additional items to adorn our new flat. It was now fully furnished and ready for occupation. We arranged the things I had brought along—a tiny dry branch of a tree I had picked up from the side of the Grand Canyon in Arizona, a collection of pebbles from Sorrento in Italy, a fossilized fifty-million-year-old tree trunk from Madhya Pradesh, a tiny stone from Hiroshima.

Then I saw a stone boulder lying in the sun on the Pune-Bombay trunk road, weighing a ton. I thought it would be just the item needed in my drawing room. I hired a lorry and had the boulder hauled into my garage, had it cleaned and washed, and moved it right into my drawing room among the sofa sets. My visitors stood aghast looking at it and exclaimed, 'It is a beauty, where did you get it from?'

'On the Pune-Bombay highway, out in the wilderness, weathering the seasons for thousands of years,' was my reply.

*

I had put in fifty years with the *Times*. But it still it did not seem long! In fact it looked as if only the other day I had stood before the formidable art director Professor Langhammer asking for a job. This illusion was largely due to the work condition I enjoyed in the *Times of India*. The proprietors of the company and all my colleagues ungrudgingly accorded me the freedom I needed as a cartoonist. They never refused a request I made regarding my travels abroad or locally, or in any matter concerning my professional needs. On the whole the deference and respect shown to me by one and all over the years made the time pass by unnoticed.

The management of the *Times* sensed my intention to retire, and somehow believed that the newspaper would not be the same without my cartoons. They said that by all means I could enjoy my well-earned retirement in Pune and also continue to work for them from there! In the computer age, with scanners, modems and other such technological devices available, it would be no problem at all, they assured me. I could transfer my cartoons to Bombay in no time once I had completed my cartoon for the day. Soon all this electronic equipment was installed in my room in Bombay, so that I could learn to handle them once I retired and shifted to Pune. A man from the computer room came to teach me to press various buttons on the units. But my progress was slow. I could not pay attention to it fully as I had to concentrate on my cartoons.

But my desire to shift to Pune soon began to flag with the arrival of Mahalaxmi, my granddaughter!

At first the gurgling she made and her smile held me in thrall. I made several rough sketches of her lying on the floor and kicking her legs. Our meticulously clean and orderly drawing room was now cluttered with a tiny mattress, pillows, bottles of milk and baby clothes.

Soon this space was invaded by musical toys, trains, cars, any number of teddy bears, monkeys, Mickey Mouse and his friends of all shapes and sizes. Then our fourteenth-century bronze Nataraja, seventeenth-century stone Hanuman, antique temple bells and curios gathered from all over the world had to be shifted to a safer place because Kutila, that is Mahalaxmi, otherwise known as Baby, Rani, Papu, Remanika, Sweety, Doll . . . had begun to toddle around, grabbing our precious items to include them among her collection of teddy bears and Donald Ducks!

It was fascinating to watch her grow. I wondered how I had ever been able to live all these years without her presence in our house. She was constantly in my thoughts, regardless of where I was or what I was doing, whether I was at work or at a cocktail party. Observing her from a corner provided me with all the entertainment and companionship I needed, and also a mysterious sense of being reborn. This precious child has added a new dimension to my life.